A TIME TO COMMUNE

A TIME TO COMMUNE

JUSTIN MERMELSTEIN

LuBelle
Publishing

for *humanity*

"History, despite its wrenching pain, cannot be unlived, but if faced with courage, need not be lived again."

— *Maya Angelou*

"How fortunate for governments that the people they administer don't think."

— *Adolf Hitler*

ONE

Alf, sy's pug, jumped down from his bed and sniffed the floor a bit. Sy rubbed his eyes and sat up at the edge of the pillow-top, queen-sized mattress, pushing away the fluffy comforter with the orange-striped duvet cover. The carpet was plush under his feet. He wiggled into his memory-foam slippers. The sun glowed through his window and onto the desk, illuminating the face of a digital clock, making it hard for him to read the time. He reached for his phone on the nightstand, and it read XX:XX.

"The hell?"

A text buzzed through. It was from his brother, Jacob: *On our way soon.* It buzzed again. Then again. Again. Again.

Sy shot up onto his feet. Another buzz. The intercom outside. Monthly announcements. On a Sunday? The occupants of the buildings were emptying into the courtyard—a semblance of a courtyard, at least, as it was built in the center of the square-shaped internment camp. Each building occupied a corner and contained eight rooms, four per floor.

About fifty people, almost the entire camp, had the same expression on their faces—why today, and what the hell could this be about? But before they could wonder any longer, the Star-Spangled Banner blared through the speakers. Not one hand on a chest, nor a hat removed. A man from Building 7, George, spat on the ground, as he did every announcement. Every anthem.

"Sunday, December 21, 2025."

"Yeah, no shit," another voice hollered. Amy, from Building 7, as well. Shy at first, jaded and fed up a year later.

"Eh, I didn't even know the date," someone else said.

"We hope this message finds you well."

Sarcastic laughter arose, followed by a low chatter. "Shut the fuck up!" CJ yelled, quieting the crowd.

"As you know, the Loyalist Party is a party of faith and leadership. We are a party of honesty, devotion, and integrity. We understand that, in your pasts, you have not been devoted to your country. In many cultures and nations, this is a crime considered treasonous. But that doesn't mean things can't change for you here, in the great United States of America. Life does not need to be this way for you.

"The Seven Levels of Rehabilitation program is a huge success. We are reacclimating so many people and will continue to do so until every single willing person has been reintroduced to society. We'll be having SLRs the week leading

up to the New Year. If you are interested, please speak with a trooper who can see to it that you're interviewed promptly.

"Life is good when you take pride in your country. Times are changing, and it's a world you'll want to be a part of. The economy is booming, unemployment is the lowest it's ever been, and we've made tremendous strides uniting people from every corner of this great nation. Thank you for your consideration, and we hope you'll make an attempt at reconciliation.

"And may God bless America!"

The speakers cut with a pop.

"Reconcile my black ass," said Reef, who lived in Building 8 and was Sy's closest friend on the compound. "Shortest one in a while."

"Surprised they weren't sucking their own dicks any harder," said CJ.

Chandra had no free hands to cover six-year-old Sejal's ears, what with four-month-old Siva in her arms. The family returned inside.

CJ put his arm around Sy's shoulders. He was taller than Sy by a good three or four inches, and prematurely white-haired. Sy liked to joke the constant wheels turning in his engineer brain pushed all the melanin out of his originally auburn. He was in his early 50s, but his youth-like demeanor and good genetics kept him young in the face and body. "You look wiped, buddy," he said.

"I drifted to sleep for a little while. I don't even remember sitting down."

CJ dropped his arm and put his hands in his

pockets. "How popular do you think the SLRs have become?"

"Some of the new prisoners . . . maybe. Not too many, if I had to guess. Solitary confinement and torture aren't popular alternatives, turns out." The sun peeked through the clouds. It felt good against the back of Sy's neck. "It's all fucking hearsay, anyway. God knows what goes on in those things. It could be even worse."

CJ adjusted his glasses. "Think Giancarlo got out?" After all, he'd been gung-ho about telling the troopers whatever the hell they wanted to hear just to get himself on the list.

"Probably dead, like the rest of 'em."

"Not a chance, huh?"

Sy looked at CJ and chuckled, not sure if he was serious.

"Yeah, I know. I guess. But maybe I don't know. Maybe *you* don't know?"

"I know." Sy turned to walk back to Building 8. "*Everyone* knows. He stopped and pointed to Marlon Sr.'s remains. "Go that way. Might as well go out the way you want."

Sy had watched as fifteen-year-old Marlon Jr. was shot in the face through the prison security fence for telling an officer to "fuck off." Each gap in the rectangular slats was three inches by two. The tall, thin son-of-a-bitch Reef had nicknamed "Stretch," drew his weapon, shot through that tiny space, and holstered. One of the rare troopers who wasn't a complete joke with a weapon, but he wasn't necessarily Clint Eastwood, so said Reef. Sy wasn't sure what scared him more: a skilled gun-handler or a maniac with no self-control. The troopers ran from one end of the spectrum to the other.

Marlon Sr., the boy's father, planned his own revenge. Though the LOTs—the nickname the tenants (and *tenants* were what the Loyalists called the prisoners) had given the *Loyalist Organization Troopers*—were known to drive around in twos and threes, there were single-occupancy rounds at times as well. Marlon Sr. had to have known it was a suicide mission, but that was irrelevant. He had been dead the moment Marlon Jr.'s limp body hit the ground.

Sy and some other tenants filled their buckets with water and dumped them on Junior's blood and brains. Then they used a broom to sweep the remains into the buckets to be buried in a grave, dug with sticks and bare hands. The rain would wash the rest of it away.

"I'll take *him* out, at the very least," Marlon Sr. had told them all as they stared down at the freshly packed earth in front of them. Wherever there was an area of least-used, treaded ground, tenants buried bodies. "I'll make him pay," Marlon Sr. said. "I'll make him suffer."

You'll be a dead man, Sy thought. It didn't matter. Marlon Sr. bawled into his hands that night and for weeks after. It echoed through the building. Eventually, the crying stopped, and sometime after that, during the LOT rounds (which were seemingly random, day and night—sometimes five to ten times a day, sometimes twenty), Marlon Sr. spotted Stretch patrolling the perimeter of their compound. Marlon Sr. climbed the fence—easy enough, due to the structure of the slats. That was, until you got to the top. Three levels of razor wire awaited you, followed by a live electrical wire, just close enough to the others that it would be impossible for even a child to squeeze through, if they had miraculously bypassed the razors. That day, Marlon Sr. didn't bypass the razors. He got past the first row, slicing himself horribly. Then he tangled in the second, where the razors shredded him. He hung on the top, suspended in a mess of torn skin and ligaments. By the time the LOT officers noticed him, he'd nearly bled out. They emptied a few rounds in him and left him to decompose. He never made a sound.

Sy stared regularly at Marlon Sr.'s skeleton, which had been hooked on the razors by his tattered clothing for more than a year now. The vultures picked him apart and a few bones fell down in the process, but plenty of him remained a shrine of death.

They buried the few bones next to Marlon Jr., and as they continued to fall through the seasons—sometimes from the wind, sometimes a curious raven, cawing and pecking for a morsel of meat it might have missed—they added them to his grave.

"Don't let your pride get in the way of a

chance of getting out." CJ shook his head. "I certainly wouldn't. Sometimes it's just gotta be about you, dude. I'm not going to lie—I'm tempted. You really think *that* was the way Marlon wanted to go out?"

"Pride?" Sy asked, laughing. "You call this pride?" He pulled at his hole-riddled, once-white thermal shirt. "How about these?" He held out his foot, displaying an old work boot with strips of material peeling back. "Fuck my pride. Fuck your pride. It's about living."

"Living," said CJ. "Exactly. It's about living. Are you living right now? Is this living? Is that the only driving force in your life?"

"Hey, man, I'm surviving."

"That's not what you said."

"It's not semantics." Sy turned again.

"It *is*. If you want to survive, I can't argue that. But if you're looking to live, well, this Groundhog Day loop isn't living. So, you can continue to try surviving here. Surviving. Not living. But you deserve to live. We all do."

Sy continued walking away. "You're right," he yelled back. "But I can live how I want, or I can live how they want." He turned one more time. "Maybe Giancarlo did get out. But do you want to risk that? Leaving your fate in their hands?" He pulled open the door and walked inside.

"And what the hell do you think you're doing by staying here, you stubborn fuck?" CJ yelled back at him.

Siva was crying again upstairs, from their second-floor bedroom. The family had arrived two months prior, after Giancarlo had supposedly been rehabilitated and given back his freedom. When the female LOT named Em, a true hardass, gave them the news that he'd gotten through, Sy didn't want to believe her. He had trouble admitting to himself that she didn't seem like the lying type.

The clock on the wall in the common room of Building 8 read just after three. It would start getting dark soon, and the temperature would plummet. He feared for the baby, as he did every frigid night.

Reef appeared from his room with some instant mashed potatoes. He handed Sy the rest, along with a half carton of milk and some string cheese. "Eat, my brother."

Sy accepted the food with a thankful smile. "Enjoy your prayer." He poured himself a cup of water in the same stainless-steel, government-issued cup he'd been drinking from for over two years now. That cup, his bed, the sink, a bucket, a wooden chair, and a hard-wired, wall-mounted lamp completed the standard set up per room.

He drank all the water and filled the cup again and sat on his bed, his back against the cold, cinder-block wall. He wolfed down the instant potatoes and milk and took his time with the string cheese, eating it like a child would, but it barely pulled apart. It was sour, past its expiration date, likely from the day it arrived, but not moldy. Not visibly, at least. Good enough. He downed the rest of his water again and refilled it one more time. Chugging water helped fill his stomach while he ate, satiating him for the time being. It wouldn't last long, but it staved off the hunger pangs.

He let his head rest on the wall and looked out of the window. The clouds had returned, blanketing the sky and sun, kickstarting sunset a bit earlier. He began to doze again until a clicking snapped him out of it. The gate. Before he could move, the LOT truck horn blared—a food delivery. Had to be. A few men and women from the other buildings had gathered already and were headed toward the truck as well.

"T-bone steaks today, I hear," said Alma, seventy-two, the resident grandmother. She stood to the side and watched as the LOTs tossed boxes onto the ground from the back of their truck. Some slid. Some dented. Some burst open. Sy jogged up and began catching them as they were tossed. So the food delivery officers threw them harder. Stretch supervised, as he often did. Lanky, with beady eyes and a tiny mouth.

Sy winced in pain as his chest throbbed with every bang of a box against his body. "Hey, Stretch," CJ called out as he, too, caught boxes. "How many camps are you assigned to?"

"Mind your fucking business. And don't call me Stretch, skidmark."

"Just curious, that's all," CJ said. "Because you're always up our asses."

"I wouldn't be up your ass if you were blonde with big tits and a twat."

"Count me out, then," Alma muttered from far enough away to avoid getting hit by a box. She stood with her coffee-colored arms crossed in front of her chest. She'd raised four children—three girls and a boy—and had a litter of grandchildren ranging from babies to teenagers. She didn't speak much of her family. That would require emotion, and Alma kept hers in check.

They caught thirteen boxes out of the twenty, which wasn't bad. They always lost some supplies when the LOTs chucked the packages in, but this was minimal. A few yogurts. A tub of ketchup.

Sy grilled Stretch as he chuckled and hopped back in his truck. The group assembled, and the tenants divvied the boxes up evenly as the LOTs pulled out of the gate. Sy watched all three latches catch at the exact same time as the door automatically closed. A stick or anything that could be wedged into the mechanism would be enough to prevent it from catching. Maybe then the gate could be pulled open, with enough strength. Or maybe then the cameras that faced the front of the complex would provide the LOTs back at their headquarters a front-row seat to an execution.

Once inside, the tenants separated the boxes according to food type. Perishables, shelf-stable, and so on. Some things were brought out front to reside in smaller boxes, dependent on the weather. When it was cold enough and supplies were kept outside, the tenants layered boxes on top of each other to try to prevent anything from getting into the food. The only things that really got through the slats in the gates were small rodents or birds, neither of which would be able to burrow through in the small amount of time someone wasn't checking on the supplies. Nor did the rodents have much interest in being out in the cold. They cared more about getting inside, where it was warm, and going for the food stored there.

Paper plates and plastic utensils came with the food deliveries, which typically happened once a week-ish. Very ish. Everything was divvied up evenly. They figured it out quickly after early bullies and wannabe alphas attempted to monopolize the rations and had the tar beaten out of them by the mothers and fathers of the group. That situation had sorted itself out in short order, and routines and standards were established.

Mothers and young children came first, no questions asked. Then the remaining mothers, older children, and fathers—unless they were single fathers, then they took the place of the mother. Then the solitary tenants. Married, in a relationship, no matter. Unless you had children, you were considered solitary. And that's the way it was and the way it worked. Sy didn't develop the foundation of the system, but he had helped hone it and shape it along with the current crop of tenants from all four buildings of their personal complex.

Each building received enough food to get the accounted-for tenants through the week based on 1,500 calories a day. That included young children, babies, and so on, which naturally created leftover food, resulting in a stockpile at almost all times. Whatever was available to eat afterward would either be offered for seconds, dependent on stock, or more likely preserved for later. This was necessary, since some weeks, food trucks were either late or missing calories, or never showed up at all. The system kept things afloat and morale higher.

Whatever could fit in the mini refrigerator did. The rest stayed on the table in the common room or in the tiny closet in the common room, the one that contained nothing but a broom, for the tenants to play housekeeper, a steel basin, and a small shelf. On that shelf was an "emergency" kit, containing a small (and since-used-up) first-aid kit, an EpiPen, a flashlight, a box of latex gloves, and two safety blankets, also known as a "fucking travesty," as CJ once yelled to a LOT. "They cost ten bucks a pop, you cheap fucks. Can't we all get one?"

"Take it up with management." This one chuckled. He was fat and cocky, and they called him Fatty Arbuckle. CJ was lucky that was all that he said. Lesser aggressions were punished with far-worse repercussions. Fatty was certain to remind him of that while swinging his telescoping baton in a circle like a cop from the fifties. "Don't forget"—he pointed at the cameras attached to poles around the grounds—"I see you when you don't think I'm watching. I know your every move. This is my territory, fuckhead."

The foodstuffs were labeled by day and expiration date using colors of torn fabric placed in front of the piles. Anything left over from the previous week was added.

At first, the tenants feasted on the previous week's leftovers until, one week in particular, a shipment didn't arrive. The pain in their stomachs after day five of eating canned corn was enough to fight the urge to binge on anything after that, no matter how plentiful it might've seemed.

Sometimes, that meant food spoiled in waiting. You either ate three- or four-day-old food, or you didn't eat. Moldy bread and cheese had to be consumed—the tenants just cut off the gross bits. You adjusted.

"Always with the rice cakes," Reef said. "Always the damn rice cakes." Not even a sprinkle of salt on them either. They tasted like Styrofoam but were harder to swallow. Sy dipped them in water. Others crumbled them and added milk, like cereal.

"At least it came," Sy said.

"Amen," said Mateo. His matted hair was greasy and looked like a single dreadlock, which was impressive for a Spaniard with fine hair.

"You need to wash that mop," Sy said.

"You're grossing us out." He pulled a can of baby formula from the back of the table. It had been there since the last shipment and now had a newer one next to it. It surprised him that they were aware enough of a baby on the premises. Previous mothers had to breastfeed or their babies simply didn't eat. But it wasn't the first time certain LOTs kept a particular eye on things. Figuring out which ones were decent human beings was the hard part.

Sy warmed some water and mixed in the formula, stirring the powder until smooth.

"Chandra?" He knocked after climbing up the steps. He waited for an answer before looking in. "May I come in?" he asked from outside of her door, careful not to look inside.

"It's okay," she said. He could barely make out the words through her sing-song Hindi accent. He smiled down at Sejal as he entered, who was playing with paper dolls she had managed to make out of food packaging material. "And who are these supposed to be?" he asked, squatting down, his long, jet-black hair hanging over his shoulders, half of it dangling toward the floor, half down his back. You had two choices while detained: attempt to crop your hair close with whatever sharp object you could manage—which just did more damage, as nothing was sharp enough to easily shear off hair—or let it grow long. Most male tenants attempted the former while their hair was still short from the mandatory buzz cut upon entering the Loyalist warehouses. That only lasted for a short while. Sy had spent more than two years in Building 8, but he made his decision within a month, after Reef sliced open his scalp with a sharpened rock while trying to use it in the same way one would a straight blade. Desperate times called for desperate measures. Only once, though.

"This one is Mommy, and this one is Daddy," Sejal said, holding up her dolls. "Daddy isn't here, though."

Sy looked up at Chandra. She shook her head disapprovingly.

"Daddy is . . ." Sejal hesitated.

". . . probably doing the same thing we are," said Sy.

She kept her eyes locked on her prized dolls.

"Have you guys eaten any breakfast yet? It's still warm."

"Sejal has, yes. I am not very hungry." She hadn't been eating well. Stress. Anxiety. Shyness. It showed in her frailty. She'd lost weight during her short stay, and her lack of nutrition was evident in her son's feeding. He fussed with her nipple more and more over the weeks.

Sy held out the cup. "I have some formula here. I know you said you were only breastfeeding, but from the sound of Siva, he's having a rough go, no?"

The last time he tried this, she had staunchly objected. "He will only be breastfed," she had said. "I will not let my baby be poisoned by these sick men."

But the formula cans were always sealed thoroughly, and Sy had even downed a cup of it himself right in front of Chandra to prove it was safe. The overpowering taste of iron triggered his gag reflex, and he had to swallow repeatedly to keep it down. It was like licking a rusty nail.

This time, Chandra seemed a bit more receptive. Relenting, really. "We have no bottle," she said.

"Maybe we can drip it onto his lips. Or even on your nipple as he feeds?" he asked. "It's about body temperature now. It won't burn you."

She took out her breast and led the nipple to the baby's mouth. He latched ferociously. Chandra winced, her skin clearly sore from the baby suckling harder and harder, desperate for milk. Sy took a spoon and handed it to Chandra. She scooped some from the cup and carefully dribbled it over the top of her breast and down onto the top of the nipple, meeting the baby's top lip. It slowly seeped into the infant's mouth. She dribbled more and more until the spoonful was gone. A pool had formed under Chandra, but no matter. Siva eased on the nipple a bit as the taste of the vanilla and cast-iron formula met his throat. Another spoonful. One after the other. He gobbled it down feverishly. Sy finally left the cup and spoon with Chandra and smiled at her. "I'll get you some food. And maybe someone has a bottle somewhere. Perhaps next door at 1-4. Doubtful, but we'll see. We can have someone toss it over the fence, and we'll boil it to sterilize it."

"Is it dairy?" Chandra asked.

"Soy," Sy responded. "Once your milk comes back stronger, you can ease him off it. There are two big cans downstairs. One is still sealed, and I'd have no problem testing it for you again." He certainly did have a problem with it. "You'll be set for a while. Get yourself healthy. I'm going to have Dr. Joseph come take a look at you. Is that okay?"

"Yes," she said, hesitantly. "Can he check Sejal too? And Siva?"

"I'm sure." The sheer, dumb luck of having a doctor brought to their compound was rarely questioned. Only appreciated.

"Thank you, Sy."

The desperation had become too much, and she had clearly broken. Everyone breaks eventually. Some take longer than others. And everyone has a story of that breaking point. Some discuss it. Some don't. Sy didn't talk about his much. Only when necessary, when it made sense. When someone struggled to come to terms with their situation, much like he had.

The light from the speaker pole, so dimly and vaguely illuminating his bedroom, was driving him mad. What was at first, to Sy, a temporary shelter, was no longer that. And he knew it for the first time. The thought had crossed his mind before, but he'd finally accepted it. That acceptance made him sick, and he threw up into his bucket until his dinner was emptied. It might've been spoiled cold cuts, really, but the thought of permanence on the compound forced the vomit out, regardless.

He wiped his mouth with the back of his hand and collapsed onto the floor, his back against the frame of the bed. He rocked forward and slammed himself into the frame again. It hurt. He wanted it to hurt. He wanted to wake up. He wanted to fall asleep. He wanted to escape, any way he could. But he wasn't going anywhere, and that notion hardened in his brain like a scab.

He tried to cry but instead hyperventilated. He stood, panicked, looking for any way out. Not out of the room. Not out of the building. Out of himself. Out of his new life. Out of life, all together. He stumbled and kicked over his bucket of vomit, and it splashed onto the wall and floor.

Help, he thought, to no one in particular. *Please help. Anyone. It can't be real. It can't. It* can't.

He was in limbo—and that's exactly what they all called it. *Limbo*.

He dragged himself up onto the bed and pulled the blanket over his shoulders. It was ragged already, having been used by someone else before him. He pulled at the orange threads until the blanket fell apart some more. Didn't take much effort. It was tattered and worn and of terrible quality, barely even functioning as something that warmed. It was pure misery. The goddamn room was freezing, and this was the best they could do?

He pulled the sorry excuse for a blanket tighter around him. He lay askew on what was considered a mattress. The mat, perhaps a few inches thick and placed across a steel tray bolted to the cinder walls of the modular cell, contained a built-in pillow, essentially just a thicker lump for a head to rest. Not ideal for a stomach sleeper. Or a side sleeper. Or an anything sleeper. But it was that or the concrete floor, and when you're tired enough, you sleep. Even when your back barks. Or your hips. Or neck.

Sy had never been to prison. Never even been arrested. An unpaid parking ticket? Once. A soggy slip of paper had blown from beneath his windshield wiper during a rainstorm before he'd had the chance to grab it. No, Sy did the decent thing—most of the time. He made the best choices he could with what he was given. A lower-middle-class life. His parents had managed to purchase their own home but only learned what being house poor was after everything began to break. But Len never gave in. He might've been on the lower end of the income scale then, but Sy wouldn't learn that of his father until he was much older and much more comfortable. Len never searched for sympathy, his pride too big, and too much. He, in rare times, might've been so angry inside that he would punch a hole in drywall when irritated enough, but only then was it obvious. And his remorse was always nearly instantaneous.

Had he realized how much help he could've used, the family might've gotten along a lot easier at first.

"No handouts," he said to Sy's mother, Rebekah, when she suggested they take some help from her brother. Pride or not, Len dug himself out. Slowly, but steadily. He didn't shy away from the hard or the operose.

Sy had a lot more of his father in him than he knew, though he had certainly never before hit life head-on in the same way Len had. His mother's ability to fly off the handle often bested him when his father's mostly level head might've prevailed, out there in what was once the real world. But after crying every bit of moisture from his body, he lay on that bullshit excuse for a mattress and made a vow to himself that he *would* be just like his father throughout his ordeal, no matter the consequences for him. Composed. In control. And most importantly, an example.

He stared Chandra in the eyes. He'd known her breaking point was coming. It had to. "You don't need to be ashamed of this—taking help isn't wrong, it's smart." Sy also didn't believe that help was always a handout, as Len had.

Chandra closed her eyes and tears trickled from the corners. "My husband is dead."

Sy shook his head. "We have a rule here. We don't consider anyone dead until we know for sure.

Are we dead? No, we're living. We're thriving. And we share our methods with each other. Wherever he is, we have no reason to believe he isn't doing the same."

"No," she said. "He's not a survivor. He withers. And he probably thinks I'm dead, and Siva and Sejal, which will have ruined him. He is dead in all likelihood."

Sy watched as Siva fell into a deep sleep. "Tell you what—I'm going to keep my hopes up. For him"—he gestured to the baby—"and for the two of you seeing each other again."

Chandra gave a short laugh and placed Siva down on the mattress, swaddled and cozy. "And what about you? Do you have hope that your family is okay?"

"I can reasonably say that my father and mother are okay. Probably not in one of these places."

"So it's hard for you to imagine anyone but yourself in trouble." She realized her English prevented it from coming out the way she intended. "What I mean is that, you have us here, and you feel a responsibility to us. But you don't have anyone out there, anyone to worry about. It's different when you are your own caretaker. Your own everything."

She was right. Did that make him selfish or selfless? He had thought of this before, but hearing it from someone else's mouth was sobering. And he realized how offensive it might be to patronize someone about a person who might mean the world to them, out there somewhere, dead. Or dying. Or suffering. Or hurting. Or thinking the same of his significant other. His parent. His child. "I meant no offense . . ."

"No, I am not offended," she said. "I know your heart is proper. And I thank you for that and for helping me. I just know that optimism can eventually crush a soul." She looked at Siva and then down at Sejal on the floor. The little girl played with her dolls, but Sy knew she was listening to every word. "We have had hard lives. Me and my husband leaving India and having no one. No money. No friends. Living with family members we barely knew. Married to each other because we were told to. Ridiculed because we did not speak the language of this country. Ridiculed for being terrorists. Towelheads. Arabs." She grunted. "I am Hindu, not Muslim. But no one stopped to ask me that. I don't wear a hijab. My husband didn't wear a turban or keffiyeh. That's not even our religion. Everyone just ridiculed. They made fun of our accent. They told me I smelled.

"But then things got better. We bought a house and lived in a suburb with other families. We felt like a part of our community, mostly. There were detractors and people who did not like us very much for 'invading' their communities, but we were accepted by most. We almost made it. And then everything changed. When he was elected those almost-ten years ago, it set off a chain reaction of events. The ridicule. It was worse than it had ever been before. The freedom and . . . and . . . confidence to say these things to us. Yet, in spite of that, we still decided to have children, and it was the worst decision. I love my children more than anything, but they were doomed to a life of terror from the moment they were conceived."

Sy shifted on his feet, his arms crossed in front of his chest. "But why bring children into a world like this? Under those circumstances?"

"Because we wanted to. We had every right to, just like every other human being."

Still selfishly motivated, Sy thought. Judged.

"I dream of those days," said Chandra, looking out of her window at the midday sun. "The days we almost made it. The anticipation of being there, on the—what's the word . . ."

"Brink?"

"No."

Cusp?"

"Yes. On the cusp of finally getting there. Being a normal person. A person who belonged. I still dream of it all the time, even though it's dangerous to let my mind wander."

"It isn't easy right now. It's terrible and inhumane. And I find my mind doing the same thing." He smiled at her, but he might as well have frowned. "But I'll be your optimist still. Because I think you'll make it. I think we'll make it. I think we'll be okay. And we started today, with this." He placed the cup of formula on the table. "We'll figure it out from here. Deal?"

She smiled. "Deal." *He is naïve,* she must've thought. "Thank you, Sy," was what she said.

"Thank *you*." He turned to leave but stopped. "There is no shame in getting food here. You and your children come first. Please."

She nodded and smiled weakly. He tousled Sejal's hair as he left the room.

TWO

A TICKING noise and then a whoosh of hot air bursting through the vents emptied Sy's head of thoughts, replacing them with euphoria and dopamine. Every few hours, the heat kicked on just long enough to bring the room back to tolerable (and to prevent any pipe-freezing, which CJ had deduced from where both the water and heat pipes ran, parallel to each other, inside the walls), where the temperature would linger until slowly plummeting back down.

Sy had nodded out while resting his head. His numb feet, layered with three pairs of socks, wouldn't allow him to fall back to sleep. He had to urinate but couldn't imagine any more warmth leaving his body. Briefly, he considered just pissing himself and basking in the warmth for the few minutes before it gave him hypothermia. At least he'd sleep to death that way.

But he didn't. He leaned over the side of the bed and pissed directly into his LOT-supplied bucket. The ever-multipurpose piss, shit, bathing, cleaning, and everything else bucket. Then he slipped on his boots and carried the bucket outside to dump.

He slid the latch and pushed open the front door. The crisp air funneled into his mouth and nose as he inhaled. Had it not felt like tiny needles jabbing the membranes of his face, it might've been pleasant. He inhaled deeply anyway, like jumping into a pool.

It had been a long time since Sy jumped into a pool. Summer of '22 in Tarrytown, New York, to be exact. A barbecue at his parents' house—the family held the Memorial Day party every year. Twenty-five years old and cannonballing into the pool, soaking anyone in range. The grill had been cooking Italian hot dogs and skirt steak, the smell wafting in the air, overpowering the chlorine stench.

Now, the smell of pine overpowered the smell of shit and piss. When Sy glanced to his left, he noticed the pile of pine wood chips that everyone at Limbo 5-8 had been waiting for. It had been poured directly to the left of the shit trench, a gouge in the earth along the edge of the compound in which they could dump their waste. Good timing, too, as George from Building 7 was dumping his own shit and piss on top of the rest of the frozen shit and piss. Sy did the same.

Most of the complex came together, all scooping handfuls of pine chips, scattering it all along the trench, covering as much of the excrement as possible. Even Alma jumped in, scattering handfuls of wood while muttering something under her breath.

The trench was not lined with any kind of material, nor was it ever emptied. Just fifteen feet deep and fifty yards long. Each Limbo had its own shit trench, and only during the winter months was the smell *remotely* bearable, especially for anyone who had been living there less than a year. Any longer than that, most would adapt a bit more. No guarantee. Though there wasn't much of a choice. Within that first year, the intros, as the tenants dubbed the new prisoners, begged for winter. Lord help them if they arrived at the beginning of spring; they'd run out of vomit long before the temperature hit 80 degrees. As it was, most of the long-time guys were gagging and heaving already.

"Suck it up," said Reef, flipping his eye-length dreadlocks back out of his face. They scattered about, not quite long or heavy enough to stay back. Reef's face was full—his nose and lips strong. His skin was dark and tight to a very muscular frame.

"Uh, what do you think I'm trying to avoid?" Mateo asked. He wore a t-shirt sleeve as a headband, keeping his own shaggy, greasy hair off his forehead.

If the tenants were lucky, like now, a truck would come through and dump a mound of pine or cedar chips at the edge of the property, just inside the fences. Everyone would haul ass to the pile and scatter the shavings over the trench, smothering out some of the smell until the wood was inevitably buried again.

Mateo walked up beside Sy. "It's too fucking

cold already."

Sy looked over. "But you still sleep like the dead."

Mateo shrugged, smiling. "I was chunkier when I came in. Mom's cooking. I'm chillier now. I'm from Cali, man. I can't handle this cold shit." Some of his baby fat had melted away after he began the LOT diet, though the young man still appeared healthy and hefty.

Sy considered his own withering arms—they were still defined, but his size had diminished, and his complexion now matched the flurries of snow falling.

The concrete bedrooms dropped into the 40s in the winter and rose to over 90 degrees in the summer. This had been confirmed after CJ ripped an outdoor, clock-like thermometer from its home midway up the same speaker pole that held the solitary courtyard light. It also housed a handful of small security cameras that pointed in different directions. CJ waited until night to do the deed, careful to approach from an angle he assumed the cameras couldn't see.

The thermometer had sat in the common room of CJ's building for a full year, and he logged the statistics four times a day—midnight, 6 a.m., noon, and 6 p.m., hiding the contraband whenever inspection came through. Which was random and sometimes didn't exist. Except for when it did. And when it did and they found something they didn't like, depending on the LOT officer, there would be hell to pay. The form of that hell was at the officer's whim. If a tenant was lucky to get a trooper simply looking to remove the contraband, they might receive a slap on the wrist. More likely, a beating harsh enough to break a few ribs or knock out some teeth. Or, in some cases, to kill you.

"I'm eating the next person who croaks," said Mateo. "I'm telling you now. I can't fucking take any more bologna and mustard sandwiches. Not even spicy mustard, goddamnit." Mateo had been in Limbo for a little under six months. He had been pulled from his parents' house in San Diego as his mother screamed from her husband's arms. She was hysterical to see her only child, twenty-three years old, being tossed like an animal into the back of a van. But his father knew there was no stopping it. Many had tried. All had failed, even if not right away.

It was flurrying just then, but nothing stuck, which was rare for this time of year in Wyoming. They were somewhere in Fremont County, by their own rough estimates—mainly gleaned from other tenants and word of mouth. The snow seemed to stick every goddamn day in the winter. The ground was frozen solid, dirt no different from concrete.

"The quicker you realize it doesn't get any better, the easier it'll be." Sy bent down and picked up a pebble in the frozen earth.

"Yeah, until I'm dead."

"Possible." The ground crunched as Sy walked along the perimeter, Mateo tagging along. "If this winter is like the one two years ago," Sy said, "we're all in deep shit."

"That your first?"

Sy nodded. "Hell of an introduction." The snow was beginning to taper off, as were his words to Mateo. The truth was, he still worried about Chandra's baby. It was too cold, and she wasn't eating enough. *She continues that too long, and that baby will be stiff by the new year,* he thought.

Mateo's shoulders dropped. He looked down and then back up. "What's the date, anyway?"

"The twenty-first."

"Well, shit, I haven't gotten you anything for Christmas yet."

"I'm a Jew," Sy said dryly.

"There goes your brand-new bologna and yellow mustard sandwich." He thought. "Wait, is bologna kosher?"

"I don't really give a shi—"

A rumbling echoed. The gate, again. The only access to Limbo 5-8.

"New intro," said Mateo.

Sy shook his head. "Intro*s*," he corrected. He tossed the pebble at the fence. It clanked off the metal and stayed in the compound.

The van came to a halt just inside. Four LOTs exited the vehicle, batons and pistols holstered until a few tenants made their way out of their respective buildings.

"Stay back," a LOT said, a twang in his voice.

He extended his baton fully.

"We're just here to receive them, that's all," Sy said. "Same as usual." He held his hands out in front of him. The winter wind blew his hair out of his face, and his blue-diamond eyes showed only how serious he was. "They're just scared, and we want to bring them inside. You know how we do this."

The LOT walked closer and quickly struck Sy in the stomach with his baton. Sy felt every nerve ending fire off at once, making it impossible for him to take a breath. He dropped to a knee, and the sensation evoked a memory of a childhood soccer game. He jumped for a header and another teammate's elbow caught him in the same hollow area just under the diaphragm. He writhed back and forth until he was able to suck in just enough air to cry. It was expected for him to cry at eight. Twenty years later, he remembered why. "You don't tell me how *we* do shit." The trooper was young and good-looking. Clean-shaven—rare in these parts—hair longer and tucked behind his ears underneath his black cap, complete with gray fatigues, black tactical vest, and combat boots. Sy could see this man's massive build under his clothes.

"Wasn't . . . telling you how to do anything." Sy gasped. "Just meant you know why we're collecting the new ones." Reef put an arm around Sy, urging him backward.

"Release them," the LOT commanded. The van door opened, and a woman was pushed out by another trooper's boot. She slid off the back of the van and fell on top of the sack she carried.

The sacks were the only things intros were allowed to bring with them. Generally only clothes were allowed to be packed, but some things were overlooked when run through the x-ray scanners at the warehouses. Paperbacks, provided they were fiction or not of anti-government ilk, were generally allowed through, as were certain medications with proper explanation. No electronics, no photographs, and limitless other *nos*. Some managed to sneak things by, but the cost was high if you were caught.

The woman used her sack to support herself and didn't hit the ground. Tears streamed down her face, though she remained stoic. Her age was difficult to decipher in her condition, but she couldn't have been more than in her mid-twenties. Her brunette hair was greasy and hung in strands on her face, not quite long enough to be tied back. She wore a shawl over her shoulders and an old blue sweatshirt beneath that. A pair of gray sweatpants, wet from the looks of them, flared out over black flats. Certainly not Wyoming-in-the-winter wear.

Sy pulled away from Reef and made a beeline for her. Reef reached out but whiffed on Sy's white thermal shirt. "Sy, come on, man," Mateo said. "Let her come to us. We'll help her that way."

He ignored them and approached the woman. The LOTs said nothing, just watched as Sy helped the woman to her feet, grabbing her canvas sack—her livelihood—in his other hand. It was small, at most the size of a backpack, and she likely had only been given fifteen minutes to pack once notified. Most people by this time had a bug-out stash somewhere in their homes: a pile of things they'd grab if and when the time came. Maybe even a fully packed sack they'd purchased on their own. "Come on. Come with me. Let's get you warm," he said softly. She sobbed and walked with an obvious limp. It was clear from her complexion and the heat radiating from her hand that she was running a fever.

"Reef, grab her room assignment card and let's get her in there," Sy said.

"You got some balls," the initial LOT said. Sy winced. It took everything to stay composed. "Just helping," he said back.

Two Latino men appeared from the van door. They managed to keep their feet as they were shoved out in the same manner as the woman before them. They were stocky, from what Sy could make out. One wore glasses. Both had their heads and faces shaved and carried their sacks on their backs. The man with glasses turned and helped a young Latina woman and her child down and out of the truck. They were neither shoved nor kicked, but their sacks were thrown at them. Both men stuck their bodies in the way to block the impact. Then the door to the van slammed shut, and the LOTs loaded back in and spun away. The gate rumbled closed behind them.

"Come with us," said Sy as the van sped down

the dirt road in a cloud of dust.

They all entered Building 8. The family—the man with glasses, the stubby woman, and their son, head also buzzed—were hand-in-hand, dazed and lost. Sy looked at them, including the man tagging along behind. "You're okay now." It wasn't a lie. Not like the LOTs cared much about you after the initial introduction, unless you did something out of line. It all really depended on how you conducted yourself. Sy had pushed the envelope outside just now. The LOTs wouldn't forget that. They never did. He knew it, too, but he wouldn't worry about it at the moment. That was for another day. He rubbed his stomach.

The single man pulled a card from his khaki pants pocket. "What does this mean?" he asked with a fairly heavy accent. Central American? His eyes were almond, but his skin light. "D8 – F2 – R6."

"That's your assignment card," Reef said. "The D8 means Dormitory 8. That's this building. There are four buildings in this complex—five through eight. F2, R6 means floor two, room six. You're right upstairs." He looked over at the other family. "Do you have your card?" The man was reluctant to answer, but pulled it from his jacket pocket. "Ramón, Cecilia, and Santiago," he read. "Building 5, floor 1, room 3. You're all right across the courtyard. It goes clockwise. Five is across, six is diagonal from us, seven to our right, and then us."

The man nodded. "Thank you." An accent, certainly, but nothing compared to the first gentleman. "Is every building the same?"

"Identical," said Reef. "Four rooms on the first floor, four rooms on the second. And this open, atrium-like design," he gestured. "Just like your favorite prison."

"I have never been," said the man.

"I was . . . kidding. Anyway, each building has this common room that we stand in. It has an outlet for the fridge and microwave, with the stairway leading up the middle and rooms on the sides. No doors on anything except the front. I guess they thought the lack of privacy would agitate us."

"Electricity is cut at 4 a.m. sharp," Reef added, "and turned back on at dusk. It's automated, so we get, at most, eleven hours of refrigeration and hot food, down to seven during the longest days."

Mothers had to improvise their baby bottles by heating the water as hot as they could in whatever bottles they were allowed and insulating them using one of the two emergency blankets.

"I don't like it," said Ramón.

Sy chuckled. "None of us do. Not much we can change, though." He thought a moment. "Not about the buildings, anyway."

Ramón was not amused. "Should we go over there now?"

"Whenever you're ready. You might want to try to warm up first." He looked down at the young boy latched to his mother's side. "Are you Santiago?"

"Yes. Santi," the boy said, his voice trembling.

"My name is Seymour. Before this place I never had a cool nickname like yours. Then Shariyf started calling me 'Sy,' and now everyone else does too." He pointed at Reef. "I started calling him 'Reef,' and now that's his name here too."

"Can I call you Sy?" the little boy asked.

"Sure can! Also, there's a little girl, Sejal, who lives in the room upstairs. She's six. How old are you?"

"I'm seven."

"Awesome! Well, she makes dolls and figures out of paper and she's pretty good at it. Maybe you guys can make superheroes. Who's your favorite?"

The little boy leaned forward. "Daredevil." He nearly whispered it.

"No way! Me too! Sejal's got a couple of crayons her mommy managed to sneak through in her bag. I'll introduce you guys later."

Santiago nearly smiled, but didn't.

Sy looked up at the child's parents. He wanted to press them. Every time intros were brought in, they would arrive with updated information, recent to their apprehension. Tenants who had arrived after the so-called rehabilitation program had begun trickled in new information about the process, and Sy wanted to know. Instead, he laid off.

"CJ keeps an eye on things over there in Building 5. He'll help you get set up. Show you to your room." He looked back down at Santi. "Want some hot chocolate before you go? It's not the best, but it's better than whatever you've been drinking at the warehouse, I'll bet." He looked up at Ramón. "Hell, even the mattresses here are better than those cots. They may be thin, but at least they don't fold in half when you sit on them."

The warehouses held hundreds of people at a time. It was there that you stayed until you were shipped out on a train to somewhere else in the country, mostly in the sprawling Midwest or Plains. The coasts were ghost towns, especially above North Carolina on the East Coast and damn near the entire West Coast.

Sy thought back to what seemed like a decade ago.

The administration had only come up with an official name a few months prior, though they'd been a separate government entity from the beginning. He'd remembered hearing that some of the force were police and former military, but that the "great civilians of this country now had a grand opportunity to fulfill their dreams of doing a service to their country by protecting it from the great evil within."

"They're inciting the violence," Sy said to his father, Len, early on.

"Seymour, the man is just trying to clean up the garbage," Len replied. "You think they're going to attack innocent people? They're going through academies, like police. They're saying it's more like boot camp, in fact. It's not some mishmash of people."

A few months later, when people were detained and brought to unknown locations, Len backtracked some. "No, I don't like it. I don't think it's right. Everyone deserves due process. They're herding people like sheep."

"Dad, we don't even know what half of these people are accused of."

A few months after that, it was obvious who they were after. It started with mostly Central and South Americans. Then Muslims. Eventually, it branched out to other minorities and then whites. They detained people for negative tweets, back when Twitter was still around. For posting on public forums and in comment sections. It made the NSA look fair and balanced in comparison. Then it was obvious they were going after anyone who voted against him. Once they dropped any pretense and simply called it an "unpatriotic act, equal to that of treason," the writing was on the wall for Sy.

Len cried when it became clear his son was in trouble. Sy's mother, Rebekah, who hadn't voted, wasn't worried about herself. She was worried about her child. And she vowed she wouldn't leave his side, that they'd have to shoot her to get to him. But the faster all Limbo construction was completed, the faster new buildings were filled. The balance had shifted from more people outside the compounds to more inside. And once they came for you, you surrendered peacefully. It was one of two choices. Binary. One, you get a room in a concrete cube. Zero, you're dead. Dealer's choice. Bullet? Curb stomp? Baseball bat? The LOTs decided as they went. Depended on how sadistic and brutal they might be feeling in that moment.

When the truck with the orange and blue lights pulled into their driveway, it all happened so quickly that no one had the chance to react. Sy's parents had come by his apartment one Saturday for lunch. He'd been eating soup at the kitchen table, his mother and father in the living room, watching TV, oblivious. The LOTs didn't tear ass to the house and screech into the driveway with sirens blaring. Just lights. No song and dance. *We're here for you. Make it easy or make it hard. Your choice.*

Sy had peered from the window when the lights became obvious through the curtains. He'd been through this drill before. Daily, sometimes. The lights reflected through a window, and he held his breath as they drove by, waiting for them to stop at his driveway.

As the two LOTs strolled to the front door, he opened his closet and stared at the shoebox that held the handgun he had acquired from a trip to Pennsylvania to visit a friend. He bought it in the event he wanted to go an entirely different route. Instead, he grabbed the sack that he'd packed months previously and threw it onto his back. Though it was nearly the end of May, he grabbed a thick parka from the closet, assuming it could come in handy, even as bedding if necessary. The reports were everywhere by that point, and he figured he'd be going somewhere in the Midwest or Mountain-state area, as that seemed to be the current state of things. He'd hoped for a Southern state due to their lack of winter, but the South came with its own set of problems—the incessant heat being the main one.

He took his phone out of his pocket and typed a message to his friends in a group chat. *"Going on vacation somewhere in the middle of the country. Keep your heads up. This will all be over soon. Tell my parents I'm sorry I didn't give a proper goodbye. I didn't want them hurt."* He shut his phone off and stuck it in his pocket.

"Mom, Dad, I love you guys," he yelled across the house. "Be back soon. I won't be long." He'd already closed the front door behind him before they had a chance to respond. It was obvious he was there to comply, but one of the officers grabbed him roughly by the arm anyway, taking the sack off his back, pulling his phone and wallet from his pocket, and tossing him hard into the back of the truck, slamming the doors behind him. His head caromed off the leg of one of the benches that lined the sides of the back of the van.

"You okay?" a man asked, his Hispanic accent barely there. He had a shaved head, goatee unconnected at the sides, and intense eyes. He helped Sy to his feet.

"I'm okay," Sy said, even as the blood dripped down his temple onto his cheek. He pulled a sock off and held it against the cut. "Is it bad?" he asked, leaning in toward the man.

"A little cut. Head wounds bleed like a motherfucker, man."

There was silence as Sy watched his house fade into the distance through the gated window on the back of the truck. He braced against the bench to prevent himself from falling forward during a turn.

"Don't bother watching it disappear. It just feels worse." He held out his hand. "Jorge."

Sy adjusted the sock on the cut. "Seymour." He shook the man's hand. "Where you coming from?"

"Albany."

"Long time to be in this fucking thing." He looked around.

"Not as long as her." Jorge pointed to a tawny-skinned woman huddled into the back corner of the van. "The few hours I been here she hasn't done nothing but cry the entire time. I tried asking her a couple questions, but she didn't say anything, so I left her be, you know?"

Sy waited for the bleeding to subside, and then tucked his belongings under the bench before switching over to the other side of the truck. "May I sit next to you?" he asked the shaking woman. She only looked up at first, blinking repeatedly as if her eyes were stinging, then barely nodded. Her skin color was stunning. A shade of gold that paler women roast for days in tanning beds to try and fail (and get melanoma) to achieve. Her long, flowing brown hair was disheveled and still gorgeous. She didn't have a sack with her. She had nothing but a light sweatshirt and what looked to be a shredded piece of fabric in her lap.

"I'm Seymour. Where are you from?"

She sighed and looked out the window before turning back to him. She looked lost in thought and then, in a heavy Arab accent, said, "Piscataway . . . New Jersey."

She barely speaks English, Sy thought. "So they picked you up first, then up to Jorge, and then came back down." He used his hands to mime what he was saying.

She nodded. He tried to figure out the thought process behind it, but there was no real way to decipher their method.

"They just do this all day," Jorge said from across the van. "I read all about it. They're assigned a truck or van and round up people all day long, drop them off at the warehouse at the end of the day, and then do the same thing the next day. Day after day. They have territories."

The warehouses. Sy had heard about them. Distribution centers of sorts. They gathered up their prisoners and assigned them an internment camp. Sent them on a train or bus and dropped them off at different stops along the way.

"I'd get comfortable if I were you," said Jorge. "It's barely noon. Long day ahead of us. We'll be packed in like sardines by the time we reach a warehouse."

Jorge was right. When they finally reached the center, it was nearly midnight. It was so tight in the back of the truck that people were literally sitting on top of each other. The heat was unbearable until the door opened for someone new and a burst of air rushed in. Twice during the pickups, Sy noticed new officers. "I guess they do this shit in shifts," he said to Jorge. But Jorge was asleep, his head up against the back wall of the truck, bumping along with the ride.

The warehouse was a small, concrete rectangle. By the time they got there, everyone was practically gasping for air. It smelled horrible and felt even dirtier than it smelled. As the back doors opened, people started to stream out of their truck and the truck next to them, guided by a plethora of LOTs leading the detainees into the building at semi-automatic gunpoint.

"Where the fuck are we?" someone asked aloud.

"Harrisburg," a trooper answered. Sy glanced over at him. The man seemed out of sorts, like it was his first day on the job. He looked around nervously, a hint of "oh, shit" on his face.

It was a slow process as both the prisoners and their bags passed through state-of-the-art metal detectors and x-ray machines. For nearly an hour, the thunks and clangs of metal and other banned objects hitting the basins next to the LOTs were the only thing that could be heard, aside from crying and moaning. Whenever there was the slightest protest, there came a sharp clap, either a smack or a punch. The complaining tapered off after a few of those, and finally everyone was through.

Next was a guard with hair clippers and a folding chair. Each man sat, and his hair and face was buzzed as short as the clipper would allow. The standard for the warehouse mugshot, no matter your age, color, or religion. Sy had been appalled at the LOTs taking the most pleasure in pulling off the turbans of Sikhs and running their clippers over the hair and beards that had never been cut, never mind shaved completely. Women had to pull their hair into a tight ponytail or slick it straight back if it wasn't long enough to tie. And if it didn't stay? They were buzzed as well. Just like Alma had been.

Finally, at the last station, the microchips were implanted. Like a dog adopted from a shelter, each person was injected with a plastic chip about the size of a grain of rice between their shoulder blades. It wasn't a GPS chip, as the Loyalists wouldn't waste their money on that kind of tracking. They simply wanted to figure out where an escapee came from, if caught, and the microchips contained their predetermined locations.

There weren't enough cots for all, though Sy drew one of them randomly. "You'll only be here overnight, and you'll be shipped out tomorrow morning, so don't get too comfortable," a trooper yelled at the top of his lungs. "Keep your filthy fucking hands to yourselves and your filthy fucking feet in your shoes. Neither I nor any of my officers want to smell that shit in here. There'll be some food and water comin' round. I'd suggest you eat it all and drink up, because there won't be anything else until you get to the compounds you're assigned to. And it might take a day or two."

Sy tried doing a headcount of people, estimating sixty-five to seventy from the two trucks that had arrived at the same time. He spotted the woman from his own truck leaning against the cinder-block wall in the back corner of the room and approached her. He took her by the hand and led her to his cot, where he offered it to her. She shook her head and pulled her hand away, backing up.

He was perplexed. "This is for you. It's mine, and I'm giving it to you." Then it dawned on him. "No, no, not *with* me," he said. "For you, *alone*. You sleep here. I sleep on the floor." He fluffed out his parka and plopped down on top of it. He smiled at her and gave her a thumbs up. She smiled back and thanked him quietly.

The food served was the first taste of the bologna sandwiches, dry cornbread, and canned peas that he'd desperately need to get used to. He ate all of it, reluctantly, worried that he would be one of the extended travelers, taking two days (or longer, for all he knew) to get to his destination.

He relieved himself in the one disgusting bathroom with both a urinal and toilet, and no sink, though a gigantic bottle of hand sanitizer was available—and empty. He tried banging it upside down, to no avail. At whatever time they deemed worthy, they shut the few lights off. Though he was on the floor, Sy was just happy to be out of the truck. The benches had been so shallow that his lower back was on fire from sitting in the same, cramped position for nearly twelve hours. He stretched himself out on his parka, his head on a rolled sweater. The chorus of sounds consisted of people crying, coughing, sniffling, and moving around on their cots or the floor. Occasionally, someone would get hysterical and beg to be released. It didn't end well for any of those people. They certainly weren't let go.

Sy stared at the ceiling. He thought of his dad, his polar opposite, though he loved the man so damn much. He loved his mother, that didn't need to be said, but his father was the man who handled life. He never broke. He never wavered. He never asked for help. *At least*, he thought, *his stupid decision helped him in the end. He won't be here.*

The trains were old Amtrak locomotives. Most of the seats were busted, the dining and leisure cars stripped to empty shells. LOTs manned each and every car, and took shifts making sure no one got up. If they needed to use the bathroom, they'd have to leave the door open and have a LOT observe their actions. That was when women were assaulted and raped. Some of the LOTs would expose themselves or masturbate to and on the women. Sometimes their husbands would be a few rows away, with no choice but to watch. Their children, too.

Sy kept his mouth shut and his eyes forward. He'd be dead before he even arrived to his camp if he lifted a finger, and he knew that. So did the husbands. Most of them. All of them, except for the poor soul who jumped up and grabbed the LOT by his dick. He squeezed and pulled so hard that the LOT sprayed blood from the tip of it. He was hit on the back of his head with the butt of another LOT's gun. Then he was propelled from the moving train, off the edge of a bank that dropped a few hundred feet. His wife was made to clean up the blood and return to her seat, but not before being struck in the face with an open hand. Sy heard about this secondhand, from a passenger moved to his car in order to make more room for a few more pickups in Illinois.

The food threat had not been a scare tactic. The entire ride took more than forty-eight hours, thanks to multiple pickups, both prisoners and LOTs, and other unexplained pauses in travel. When they finally arrived at the Wyoming warehouse, they were given more questionable meat sandwiches and faucet water. Then, quicker than expected, they were loaded into trucks and shipped out to their camps.

When the LOT truck pulled up on July Fourth of 2023, Sy was shoved through the back doors. He managed to keep his footing and stumble out onto the earth. He looked back at the LOT who was responsible. He was tall, lean, and long in the limbs. Sy killed the man with his eyes.

The tall LOT grilled him back with a shit-eating grin. "What you gonna do, boy?"

Sy turned and continued walking, the group in front of him waiting for his arrival. A man, front-and-center, held out a hand. "CJ."

"Seymour."

He led Sy to Building 8, according to the assignment card stuffed into his pocket by the fucker who'd shoved him. George, the only other prisoner dropped off with Sy, was taken to Building 7 by someone else.

"Room 2, home sweet home," said CJ.

The moment Sy saw his mattress, he leaned over the sink and dry-heaved the next-to-nothing that existed in his stomach. When he was done, he apologized.

"Yeah, it's real, my friend. But don't apologize. I did the same thing. Only mine was when I saw the color of the water in the sink."

Sy's head dropped some.

"It's cleared up since then, thankfully. It's not bad, once you get used to it. At least it's new construction. Though the sweetness of the lead ground pipes is so delicious that I've forgotten how to spell my first name."

"What's CJ stand for?"

CJ paused, pretending to think. Sy laughed for the first time since his ordeal began. "Carson John. My mother liked the way it sounded and looked when she wrote it in cursive. And she loved Johnny Carson."

Sy smiled. But the smile faded after CJ left him to his new home. He was nauseated again, but he fought the vomit back.

Don't break, he thought. *Don't waver.*

But that would take some practice.

THREE

REEF LOOKED up from the sickly woman's assignment card. "You're right here in this building. Room 1, next to Sy."

The Marlons' old room.

"That's full capacity again," Reef realized, looking to Sy. More and more people. When rooms were empty, it made Sy and the rest optimistic. The fewer intros, the fewer people were being taken in. But it was still on the upswing.

Mateo led the family to Building 5 and then showed the other man, Sebastian, his room.

"She's warm," Reef said from where the young woman sat. Sy reached for her forehead, and she leaned in. "Are you sick?"

"I'm not sure," she answered, confused. "My leg hurts from where someone stepped on me in the truck. And I have a cut on my back, but I haven't been able to change the bandage."

"Mind if we get the doctor to take a look?" Sy

asked.

The woman shook her head. "There's a doctor here?"

"We're a lucky bunch in that regard—Joseph in Building 6 is a surgeon."

She looked relieved.

"What's your name?" asked Sy.

"Priscilla."

"That's lovely. It's nice to meet you."

Priscilla smiled weakly. As she blinked, she kept her eyes closed a tick longer than normal. The fever. The tears. The cold. The exhaustion. She was trying to read Sy, he could tell. Could he be trusted? Perhaps. Or perhaps the LOTs had been nice to her at first, too. They did that at times. It wasn't always a thrashing. The tactic was to gain some trust. Get people to do what they ask. *"We're not going to hurt you. This is just temporary until we get the entire situation figured out."* The situation was that they needed you to do what they asked, en masse, without revolt. Once they had you alone and vulnerable, they hit you. Stomped you. *Raped* you. They culled the herd into manageable groups, then they beat you into submission. There were too many of them and too few of you. So you agreed to anything they asked. Just stop hitting me, please. Stop throwing my food out if I don't answer quickly enough. Stop touching my body. Stop spitting on me if I have an accent and you don't understand what I say.

"This is America, you roach."

Sy shook it off. "Let Reef take you inside your room so you can sit and relax. I'll go find Joseph."

Buildings 8 and 5 were fully occupied, Sy thought as he strode along. Building 6 was two short of capacity, and 7 was five-eighths full. That left five bedrooms out of thirty-two. Not the most occupied ever, but close. It was why he had assumed there'd be more than one intro in the van.

The snow started again, dusting the ground. The empty branches of the trees outside the compound swayed in the stiff breeze. Sometimes they clacked together or just creaked ominously, dry and in need of a good, healthy source of food—sun. Warm, lovely sun. The flakes pelted his eyes as he squinted his way to 6. He pulled open the door, but not before stopping to glance at the mountains in the distance. It wasn't a view he'd ever seen in New York State. Not of this magnitude, anyway. And despite his circumstances, Mother Nature eased the pain at times. The view could stop an anxious mind in its tracks. But only briefly.

"Joseph, you around?" he asked, closing the door behind him.

"In here," a voice answered from the first room to the left. Joseph was reading a small paperback that he'd traded with someone from the same building.

"A few intros just showed up. One's not doing so well. She has something going on with her back. A cut or a gash. Might be infected, because I think she's got a fever. She was stepped on at one point, too. She's limping mighty hard."

Joseph closed his book and dropped it on the windowsill. "Is she lucid?"

"Yep. Enough."

Joseph came from a long line of doctors, great-grandfather on down. His wife was a dentist. She was likely, or so he hoped, helping out at some other Limbo. The Ohio couple had been split while they were packed onto the train to Wyoming. It wasn't that the LOTs separated you on purpose—they just didn't care about splitting any group to fit more people in a car. Sometimes you were regrouped at the warehouse. Sometimes a car was emptied and the others weren't. No conductor was stopping the train for a hysterical passenger. The LOTs didn't pay them for that. They'd have the conductor's head on a stick. So the trains chugged on, destroying the lives of parents and children and husbands and wives in their path.

Joseph was the eternal optimist. He refused to believe this would last forever. And when it was over, he'd find his wife again. He bragged about her all the time. Taller than him, blonde hair always tied up in a tight bun, cheekbones for days. She was a compassionate dentist, according to Joseph, necessary to be married to someone like the doctor. It oozed from his pores. He felt an obligation to the tenants immediately.

Sy certainly didn't know the percentages, but

he'd venture a guess that the mortality rate was something brutal in Limbo. The elderly barely made it out of the train and rarely lasted long at the dorms if they did. Anyone who needed medication was done in once their prescriptions ran out. Sure, you could make requests, but they'd rarely show up, and when they did, there was never enough. And it wasn't as if the LOTs didn't have the supply. Rumor had it that they'd bought from pharmaceutical companies in bulk, making sure the corporations weren't going bankrupt after losing a large chunk of their money flow.

Some folks would stretch whatever prescriptions they had in hopes they'd get help before going into diabetic shock or their high blood pressure gives them a stroke. The medication might eventually show up long after a tenant was dead, so Joseph would store them for whoever else might come through in need. A supply of antibiotics, painkillers, insulin, and other medications was stockpiled, but one outbreak of something nasty or a new diabetic tenant and that stockpile dwindled hastily.

Joseph grabbed a few different antibiotics from under his bed and stuffed them into his jacket pocket. He took an old t-shirt from a clean, folded pile.

Priscilla was in a ball on the mattress of her new room. She drank microwave-warmed, tepid water and wrapped two blankets around herself. One was LOT-issued, the other was one of the two emergency blankets. She'd pulled her knees tight against her chest, her arms wrapped around them. The shawl and two blankets covered her up to her cheeks. Her black flats poked out from under the blankets.

"Priscilla, it's Seymour from earlier," he said from just outside the door. "I have Dr. Joseph here. Can we come in?"

"Sh—sure." She audibly chattered.

"Hi, there. I'm Joseph." He entered the room and knelt down next to the bed. "Can I take a look at your back?" he asked. "I know you don't want to take those blankets off, but we need to get you clean dressings. You'll feel much better after that. Also, this emergency blanket is too heavy for your fever when the heat is on. If it gets below a normal temperature, you can use it. Otherwise, it's only going to keep your fever higher than it needs to be and will make you feel worse." She sat up, and Joseph helped her unwrap the blankets. Sy sat on the room's wooden chair. "Where are you from?" Joseph asked. He lifted the bottom of her sweatshirt and she hissed. The dressing had shifted, and the sweatshirt material stuck to the dried pus and fluids leaking out of her.

"Vermont," she said through tears.

"Vermont! And you're chattering? This should be like home for you!"

She managed a weak chuckle. "Not . . . my idea of a vacation."

"You're gonna love it. We have heated pools, an eighteen-hole golf course, spa, whatever you want." Joseph microwaved a cup of water to near-boiling and dropped the fresh gauze in. He then pulled the old dressing off steadily and meticulously, careful to avoid hurting the woman even more. He worked efficiently, trying to abstain from keeping the wound open for too long, Sy gathered. He studied the doctor's expression intently, but Joseph let on absolutely nothing. Stone-faced.

"Is it bad?" she asked quietly.

"It's certainly infected. I'll clean it, wrap it, give you some pills, and we'll see if it clears up."

She nodded, and something resembling a smile spread on her face. Possibly relief. Probably the first she'd had since being taken from wherever she was. Warm. In her home. Maybe a husband. He looked at her left hand. No husband. Not unless the ring had fallen off or been stolen (the LOTs were prolific thieves as well). Could've been with her family. A roommate. Alone.

"This is going to sting a bit, but it won't hurt long."

She squeezed the mattress again, and the doctor bent her forward a bit more. He pulled a piece of gauze from the cup, holding the fabric by the corner. He draped it over the cut and she gasped and tensed, then relaxed. Joseph then used the gauze to clean the wound. After, he tore his folded t-shirt into strips, and then pulled one of the pill bottles from his jacket and removed a capsule. He dumped most of the remaining water into the sink and left less than a teaspoon at the bottom. He pulled the capsule apart and emptied the contents into the cup and stirred it with a plastic fork he produced from his other pocket. Once it made something of a paste, he applied it to the wound with a piece of t-shirt then added more to a folded-up strip and placed it against the gash. He wrapped the remaining strips around Priscilla's torso and tucked the flap in and knotted it around the others. "Try to keep this in place. You can wash your body if you have the energy but leave this alone until the meds are in you twenty-four hours." He held out a pill and then refilled the cup with tap water. She took it from him and swallowed it. Sy noticed she'd stopped shivering.

"How's the leg?"

"It hurts," she said. "But I'm okay. I can manage."

"At the hip?"

"On my thigh."

"Can you straighten your leg for me? All the way out."

She extended her leg in front of her and moved it side to side.

"It's not broken." He palpated it through her pants. "They kick you? It's swollen."

"I was stepped on in the train, I think. I nodded off against the side of the car and my legs were crossed in front of me, crisscross. We stopped short and a large man stumbled back on me, and I think that's when it happened. At least, that's when I started to feel the pain. It startled me awake."

"A bone bruise or strain can last a while. A tear can be even worse than that. But we really have no way of knowing, especially right now. We'll keep an eye on it. But we need to take care of this infection first, as it's more dangerous. Relax as much as you can." He cleared his throat. "Sy will get you acclimated. He's one of the old men on campus."

"A regular Van Wilder," Sy said.

Joseph laughed emptily, with no clue what Sy was talking about.

"'Happy Days'? 'Animal House'? Silent movies? Better?"

Joseph flashed him the finger.

Sy redirected his attention to Priscilla. "I'll leave you be, but I'm right next door if you need anything. I wish we had some fever-reducers, but the last outbreak drained us of everything. Meds come so few and far between."

Every once in a while they'd get some saint from outside who'd sneak them a few supplies. It was pretty rare, as *no one* wanted to be caught on camera. They'd get random items like pain relievers, rubbing alcohol, pencils, matches, etc. The matches were great, but they couldn't exactly create a bonfire inside, and the moment a fire was spotted outside, LOTs would storm the buildings and put the fear of God in them. If they were lucky.

By the time Sy realized Priscilla didn't necessarily need to hear any of this, she had already fallen asleep against the wall, her adrenaline crashing and the days of exhaustion catching up all at once. He helped her to the pillow and covered her back up with a lighter blanket at the doctor's behest. He walked out into the common room and checked the temperature in the building. Seventy-one. The heat had fired on at about midday, and the bright sun helped keep the temperature comfortable.

He took a deep breath. It was still early, and the day had already been long. The quiet was welcome.

#

DARKNESS, ASIDE from a glint of light from the waxing crescent moon and the dim glow from the lamp atop the speaker pole in the courtyard. Otherwise, darkness.

Sy drifted back to sleep as his feet thawed. Sleep was almost always empty, devoid of any memorable dreams, aside from a few rogue ones. If he ever remembered them, they were likely of his mother and father, eating dinner at home and watching television. The mundane, everyday things that he missed the most. The big life events of his past were the last thing he reminisced about. His graduation from Stony Brook University, class of 2019, miserably stuck out on Long Island, some six years prior. His first big job, which would become his career—pulling apart damaged hard drives and plucking as much information off them as possible for distraught customers paying through their noses for a fraction of the data they sought. It paid for his first apartment, back home in Tarrytown, New York. Though it might have been anecdotal, it seemed most of the tenants felt the same, albeit a few outliers who wanted nothing more than a porterhouse steak or a week on a Caribbean island. And Sy couldn't blame them for their desires, either. How could he judge someone for wanting freedom? Whatever freedom they desired was their choice. Their daydream. Their fantasy.

But that was all it was.

He dropped his legs off the side of the steel shelf and onto the concrete floor and stretched. The cold permeated the cotton layers of his socks before he had a chance to slide on his standard-issue rubber slippers.

Sy meditated in his own ways. He made himself nice dinners out of whatever was available to him and took his time to eat and enjoy the fact that he could, in fact, eat. He read the limited selection of books available, some of them more than once. It could be worse, he often reminded himself, yet only in those moments could he really believe it. And when he maintained that mindset, it kept him fighting. Kept him motivated. Motivated to continue work on things like the map drawings he had been crafting. He based them on what he could visually identify and what other tenants had told him about what they'd noticed or about what they'd learned on their trips to Limbo. By getting their accounts, he could compare them to other tenants and come up with a realistic lay of the land, distance from warehouses to Limbo, and so on.

He had pencil-sketched himself a crude map on multiple brown bags and cardboard from the food packaging at first. They'd managed to decipher the ten Limbos in the immediate area. The way they figured that out was because, beyond what they could see from their lot, CJ, the madman he could be, decided to climb out of the second-floor window and up to the pitched roof. He clawed his way to the top after sliding back down a few times (and nearly off the edge to a guaranteed limb break of some kind, if not worse). Some of the tenants watched out for LOTs, and they timed it for sunset in the middle of summer.

It took them two hours to get him down. He perched atop the roof and refused to move. Sy was afraid that any longer spent in that world might be enough to steal his mind. Or worse. It was high enough to end it, as about a dozen people had done in the five years the structure had been there.

Each camp was nearly exactly the same as the next, theirs included, as far as they could tell, but their locations on the land snaked in and out, almost as if the architects had purposely hidden them from each other.

CJ had also averaged everyone's answer when asked how long they felt they'd been in the LOT truck or van from the time they left the train or buses or local warehouses and got into trucks or vans. He did this to get a rough distance. A lot of the time, the tenants were too petrified to realize how long they'd traveled, but a few of the cooler heads were able to give a rough estimate. Very rough. But people came from too many different directions on different modes of transportation to make sense of any of it. Not enough data to average anything. Not enough information to confidently make an educated guess, either.

So the copies of the maps, which Sy recreated on cleaner pieces of paper bag, were made for other tenants to provide some sort of comfort—knowing slightly where they were and what the grounds looked like. Creating them was a semi-relaxing undertaking, worth it for that alone. He slid them under his mattress when he wasn't working on them.

CJ and Reef helped with some of the calculations, CJ having a natural mind for math and logic and Reef having experience in navigation from his time in the service. Escape was something they'd all discussed briefly, but the real reason Sy worked on the map was because it made him feel that he possessed some sort of control over their situation when they could vaguely make out where they were in a world that had become foreign.

From smartphones and GPS to sketched maps. Rudimentary concepts learned in grammar school that just weren't applied in a world in 2025, or 2023 when Sy was taken away, or for a very long time before that. But a certain savvy comes into play after a few months with absolutely nothing. It's like the dust and cobwebs clear from the deep recesses of the brain that aren't used anymore because people rely on some device to do it for them. Sy started to . . . think. The parts of his mind and even body that had fallen asleep and atrophied started to redevelop. Pins and needles fired off until he finally learned to feel again. To exist from the visceral person inside.

He felt everything now. Every sense. Every word. Every breath. In a way, the map he was making might have initially been a plan to figure out exactly where the hell he was. Instead, it had become a sort of new world. Something he and the others were discovering like the explorers of some foreign land. It not only helped pass the time, but it lent them a meaning. Sure, they'd make it easier to navigate the immediate area if they were ever to escape, but beyond that, they were up shit's creek.

Institutionalized, he often thought. *Or was this what it was like to be Lewis and Clark?*

He knew the inside now. He was no longer a part of the world that had fallen apart in front of his eyes and abandoned him and everyone else like him. Or even semi-like him. The world that allowed this all to happen.

Sy clicked off the lamp in his bedroom and collapsed back onto his mattress. He figured it was about nine. The heat continued blowing through the vent, bringing the temperature up to a tolerable level. It was only when he pulled his orange blanket up to his chin that he heard the faint sound of whimpering. At first he thought it was a child, but it was too close to him. Without turning on the light, he stood and crept to the doorway. The whimpering came again, from Priscilla's room.

The concrete was cold under his socked feet, but the building was marginally comfortable. He stubbed his pinky toe on a wooden chair in the middle of his room and nearly threw it at the wall before barely regaining his composure.

"All right over there?" Reef asked from his bedroom.

"Yep. Good," Sy responded, keeping his voice low. He finally approached Priscilla's room, but by then the whimpering had ceased. He entered and listened closely to her breathing. It wasn't labored or junky. He reached down and touched her forehead— it was perfectly cool, but she almost jumped out of her skin. She sat up and put her arms in front of her. "Fuck off! Leave me alone!"

"Priscilla, it's me, Sy. I'm sorry, I just heard you making noise . . ."

She was still half-dreaming.

"Sy, from the bedroom next door. You're in Limbo—the compound."

She slowly came to, rubbing her eyes. "Jesus." She looked around and winced a bit as the skin on her back stretched when she moved.

"I'm so sorry," Sy said. "You were whimpering in your sleep. I thought maybe you were having a fever dream and wanted to make sure you were okay."

She yawned.

"I think your fever has broken," he said, noticing the puddle of sweat on the pillow.

"That's gross," she said, blinking. "I'm sorry. Do we have any towels? I can use a shirt from my bag to clean it up."

"It's okay, don't worry." He went to his room and fetched a towel and wiped down the bed around her. She hadn't even laid a sheet, so the vinyl was easy to dry. "You're gonna want to put some material down on there. It gets cold at night." He dropped his eyes to her hands. They were shaking. She held them to try to disguise it—embarrassed, by the look on her face.

"You cold?" he asked, giving her an escape.

She nodded, reluctantly.

"We have spare blankets in the common room. Change your clothes so you don't freeze, and we'll make you a real bed."

By the time he gathered the blankets in the dark common area, Priscilla had changed into another set of clothes. "Here you go." He held out the folded blanket. "We have extras of some things. If not, we try to figure out a way to get it. Another building. Even neighboring Limbos." He looked around her room. "The sink here works all the time, though it's only cold water . . ." She nodded knowingly. "Someone went over all this with you already, didn't they?" he asked, smirking.

"They did. But thank you."

It was too dark to study her face, but she somehow seemed even younger than when she'd arrived hours earlier. "Get some rest. Don't want that fever coming back. You're in good hands." He stepped out of the doorway. "Sorry I scared you. You just had me nervous."

It was hard to tell, but it seemed a frown spread across her face.

"And I'm so damn sorry you're here. But we'll take care of you until you get better. And we're all in it together until this is all over."

Sy canvassed the building one more time, checking in every bedroom. Most were asleep, but Reef was saying his final prayer of the day. *Isha'a*, Sy remembered. It was the only one he remembered by name, mostly because Reef was almost always the last one awake with Sy. And the first one up.

"Mr. Seymour," Reef said quietly.

"*Mr. Anderson*," he mocked. "Was I being a pain in the ass moving around?"

"Stop." He stood from his makeshift mat, an orange blanket folded in the middle of his barren room. "I'm done anyway. Allah will have to be satisfied. It's cold on the floor."

"It's cold everywhere." Sy looked out of the window of Reef's room. He stood quietly. He wanted to go back to his room and sleep but didn't have much energy to move.

"Something bothering you?" Reef asked.

Sy smirked. "Not any more than normal."

"I'll call BS."

"What makes you say that?"

"You're out on your feet," he said, putting his blanket back on the bed. Reef washed his few blankets almost every day, as they needed to be clean for prayer.

"Just . . . I don't know. Can't turn my brain off."

Reef spread the blanket out. "Sleep is important."

A whip of wind shook the cheap windows and blasted a draft through the entire building. "Rich, coming from you."

"I'm learning too. We've been here, what, almost three years?"

"Yeah," Sy agreed.

"And you and I both know that the only way anyone has made it through is by being a little bit selfish."

"By going to sleep?"

"Sure. By taking care of yourself first, sometimes. We're all guilty of it. We take care of one another like family and forget about ourselves."

Another gust of wind curled through the gaps in concrete and found its way up Sy's spine. He crossed his arms over his chest. "I'm not doing an SLR."

"I didn't say you should."

"You've been talking to CJ." Sy shook his head. "Not gonna happen."

"I won't push you then. I'm just asking that you think about it."

"We've all earned it. We're all going through this. Why not you? Why not the both of us, then?"

"I'm a black Muslim. I'm last on the list of someone they'd let back into public. I'm last on the list of useful for them. And I can hold it down here until you or someone else can get back to get us out."

"I think you're overestimating what I can do once I'm out."

"I think you're underestimating yourself."

"That's where you're wrong," Sy said. "Because I'd drive the first sharp object I found through their necks. *I'm* last on their list, they just don't know it." He rubbed his eyes. "We don't know anyone in any Limbo who was sent back from an SLR. Are we gonna assume they were *all* successful? We don't know what happens," Sy said. "Even if the successful ones get through, what happens to the ones who aren't? Do I want to put my life in their hands even more than it already is?"

"Not many have tried, in the grand scheme," Reef responded. "And the ones who have—Jacob, Natalia, Marcus—they were clean-cut enough with the ability to connive their way through, I'm sure. Let's not pretend that just because we're all in here together that there wouldn't be a preference for your skin color over mine. Is it a death sentence? I don't know. But this is. Eventually. A year from now. Two. Whatever."

Sy didn't buy it. "That's what they want us to believe. These aren't people of their word, Shariyf. These aren't people. Those three are probably dead."

"Could be. But you will one day be dead. And me. We all will. And who knows when? Will it be in here? When they stop feeding us? When they stop heating us? Why rely on their whims?"

"Do you really think I have the capacity to feign any kind of . . . rehabilitation?" Sy spat the words.

"If you're selfish enough. You want to be the nice guy who finishes last? Finishes dead? At twenty-nine?"

"Eight."

"For a few more days." Reef shook his head. "And here. Here?" Reef hugged Sy and kept a hand on his shoulder. "It's okay to be there for yourself."

"All for one," Sy said, half-joking.

"Go to bed. You're delirious."

His eyes burned from exhaustion, the kind of exhaustion that reaches down into your soul and smothers it a bit. Still, Sy lay staring at the ceiling, teeth chattering. The heat had all but escaped, and the frayed orange blanket barely covered his body. He rolled to his side, curled into the fetal position, and tried to cover himself completely with the blanket. It had been a long day. Still, a normal day. Every damn day was long and every damn day poked at the exposed nerves of his being, of all their beings. Every day took something important from them that they could never get back: time. Amongst other things. But time was the glaring, fleeting ghost. Every damn day stole a damn day.

Reef wanted him to get out. CJ wanted him to get out. What would he do out there? Out where?

He was asleep before he could finish the thought.

FIVE

A SHRIEKING laugh startled him awake. It was light, sun high in the sky, and Sy squinted through the brightness. His blanket was on the floor and one of his socks was off. Restlessness had shifted the mattress again, and the bottom hung off the steel. He stood up and nudged it back with a knee, then slipped his sock back on. He stared at his face in the reflection of the sink faucet. He was a large eyeball, then a bulbous nose, and finally, fat, Mick Jagger lips. The distortion made him laugh until another shriek snapped his head up. Sejal and Santi were chasing each other around the common room. His heart raced from the startle, and a wave of anger washed over him for it. It fleeted and he splashed his face with the icy-cold water. He reached over to the cup on the sink, filled it, and drank.

Mateo and the little boy's parents sat in chairs along the far side of the common room, enjoying the children having fun with one another. It was the first time any of them, Sy included, had seen children interacting joyfully in a very long time. The sound was refreshing. Invigorating, like the cold water. Mateo approached.

"How the intros doing?" Sy asked.

"Okay," he answered. "Alive. The boy and Sejal have been playing for hours. It's nice to see."

"They eat already?" Sy asked from the doorway.

"Did they ever," Mateo said. "I don't think we're going to be eating this week."

Sy smiled large. He finally realized why his grandmother had been so happy whenever he'd eat anything she offered. He turned around and pulled some clean clothes from his burlap sack. He layered up with a few thermals and some sweatpants. Two fresh pairs of socks felt good against his skin, and his boots felt a lot less rough with the layers protecting him. He pulled out his pail and snatched a tiny piece of remaining soap off the sink. It was too small to effectively wash the clothing. He'd have to borrow someone else's. It had been nearly a month since the last soap bars came in with the food, which meant a delivery was due soon. He wouldn't hold his breath.

Priscilla was awake when he knocked. The color had returned slightly to her pale face.

"The kids wake you up?"

"I'm used to it."

"You have any?"

"No." She paused. "No, no. Nieces and

JUSTIN MERMELSTEIN

nephews, though. I'm the youngest in my family. Lots of babysitting."

If you'd been separated from someone close to you, it was impossible to say the word "family" without your voice cracking. Priscilla had done a good job of it. "I have a nephew," Sy volunteered. "Haven't seen him since he was a baby. Long before I was sent here."

"Oh." She didn't pry, but he continued.

"My brother moved across the country when he got married. Kind of disappeared. Didn't come home much aside from holidays and whatnot. Eventually, not at all. I wish I could see the kid now. He's probably huge."

Priscilla frowned. "My sister's asshole of a husband walked out on them when she was six months pregnant," she said. "The other one is okay. Regular family. Husband's a good guy."

"So three girls?"

"Three girls," she acknowledged. "Just a brother?"

"That's it. Mom, Dad, and the two of us. I was the one who stayed back with my parents. Adam was gone the moment he graduated high school." He glanced at the wooden chair. "Mind if I sit?"

"Sure."

He sat in the chair against her wall, opposite the bed. Priscilla had propped herself up against the concrete. "He went to the Army, did six years, then got married. Moved to Cali after that. Back to where her family was from. I guess he liked her family better." He snorted. "He's three years younger than me, but we never really had much of a relationship. Just obligated love. Nothing more."

"Personality differences?"

"Might say that. Different beliefs. Values." Sy looked around. "He's not in one of these places."

"Ah." Priscilla rolled her eyes.

"Anyway, how are you feeling?"

"Better, I'm assuming?" Joseph asked, appearing in the doorway.

Sy's eyes widened. "Now that's timing."

"Better," Priscilla said. "Fever seems to have broken. I soaked the bed in sweat last night."

Joseph walked closer and extended a hand. "May I?"

She scooted to the edge of the bed and he gently palpated her throat, feeling her glands. "Still swollen. Look over at the window and open wide." He shifted over and looked as far down her throat as he could. He asked Simon to fetch him a plastic butter knife to use as a tongue depressor. "Any headache?"

"Slight."

"Remember, your fever might've broken last night, but it could come raging right back. They're funny like that, infections. May I check the wound?"

Priscilla stood, still gimpy on the injured leg. She lifted the back of her shirt and Joseph studied the bandage. Then he untied the fabric and unwrapped it from her body. It was still oozing and looking mean. Possibly worse than the day before. He pulled more ribbons of fabric wrapped in a bigger piece of fabric from his pocket, along with two packets of honey. He dipped them in steaming water. "This should help, but unfortunately we don't have much in the way of sterilizing. We ran out of rubbing alcohol some time back. Haven't gotten our hands on any since."

The doctor irrigated the wound using a cup of water and a clean piece of shirt, ripped open a packet of honey, and drizzled it on a strip of fabric, all while humming a song in a fine tune. "It's certainly not perfect, but it will help keep the area clean." He finished dressing the wound, and Priscilla relaxed back on the bed.

"Thank you," she said. "So much."

"Of course." He looked at her sitting on the bed. "Take it easy for a few days. As I said, that fever could come back at any time. We have to take it easy. I'll check on you a bit later." He disappeared into the common room.

"Honey Pie," Sy yelled after him.

Joseph popped his head back into the room, quizzically.

"You were humming Honey Pie."

"Yeah! Good ear."

Sy shrugged. "Good guess. Hell, it's been so long since I've heard music."

The doctor pointed to his head. "Always playing up here. I've got an endless catalog. My building probably hates me."

"Where'd you go to medical school?" Priscilla asked as the doctor leaned further back into the room.

"Ohio, where we're . . . I'm from. Northeast Ohio Medical University."

"Do you work in a hospital?"

"Yes. I'm a surgeon. Emergency room. Wanted to be a pediatrician, but I fell in love with fixing people from the inside." He thought for a moment. "Though, there's some more to the story. Would've been happy either way. Anyway, get some more sleep. And take the antibiotic."

"Thank you, again," Priscilla said.

The late-morning sun washed her room in light and heat. Sy left her to relax while it was comfortable to do so. He also left her a bologna-and-cheese sandwich in case she felt hungry.

Outside was more of the same as the day before. Sy surveyed the land, looking for any LOTs on foot or, more likely, in their vehicles. The LOT gig was cushy, as was the pay, so the tenants had heard. If you asked a random detainee, or even a LOT himself, you'd get figures anywhere from $50,000 to $150,000. A decent amount of money anywhere, and riches in a place like where they resided in Wyoming. None of it was likely to be true—some of the LOTs were just braggarts, prodding the tenants in hopes they'd respond and retaliate. Some of them just wanted to hurt you. Maim you. Leave you disabled or dead. But some just wanted to make a living. Provide for their family, for better or for worse. When the opportunity arose, they jumped on it, putting aside ethics and morality to provide. Ironic. Understandable. Sad.

A random tenant or two paced the courtyard, stretching their legs and attempting to delay the atrophy of muscle. One could do as many pushups and pullups as they wanted, but without the proper nutrition, it only delayed the effects. Sy was okay delaying things, so he worked out daily. He and Reef both. They did all the bodyweight workouts they could, careful not to burn too many calories. It helped, but he had begun to notice less strength mere months after his arrival to Limbo.

He did his typical rounds, circling the perimeter and then zigzagging back through the grounds. Sometimes, he'd stop and stare over at the other Limbos, close enough to see and even sometimes hear. The fences were separated by about thirty yards in between. He'd reflect on his time, and the fact that the fences had been up five years already. Five years.

The waves of people had trickled in slowly, initially. Under the radar. By the time the public understood what was going on, it was too late to do anything about it. At first, it was hard to believe. Then it was hard to avoid. Then it was inevitable. They began fleeing to other states. To other countries. They hid if they couldn't run. Sanctuary states like New Jersey and New York were steadfast for as long as possible, but they were eventually gutted from the inside out. A portion of military and law enforcement turned on its civilians. The others on the force just couldn't stop expropriation once other states sent in backup. So they either surrendered or fell in line, saving their own asses. Limbo 5-8 never held a police officer. Only a firefighter. And that was before Sy's time.

Sy stared at the roof of his building and thought, *One day, I will burn this entire place to the ground.*

He turned away and strolled up to the fence next to Building 5, which faced nowhere in particular, and was one of the very few areas that were not in plain sight of a camera. Just a thicket of bushes that had grown through and under the fence. In the far distance, the mountains climbed the sky, eventually jutting into it, sharp in some areas and rounded in others, like a mixed set of teeth.

He stepped around some dormant bushes that protruded through the fence, pulled down his waistband, and took a piss on the fence. That's when he noticed it: corrosion in the welding where some of the rungs met the pole, about two feet off the ground. And not just the start of the degradation—it had advanced enough to flake some. It was over a section of about four inches by four inches. Something in the area was weakening the joints. Could it have just been the urine? That part of the fence was, after all, his go-to outside piss spot. How had he missed it?

Sy kicked at it with the tip of his boot,

chipping away at the oxidized metal. Then he inserted his boot between the rungs and stepped with all of his weight. It didn't budge. He did it again. Still nothing. He looked around to make sure he hadn't drawn any attention, eyeballed the camera, and then reared back and stomped on the corner of the rung. It popped. It didn't look disturbed, but the crack in the welding between the rung and the pole was visible, and Sy could now wiggle it with the toe of his boot.

He stepped back and turned away with his hands in his pockets. Two minutes later a LOT truck circled the yard, four in the cab. He kept walking, right past them, pretending they weren't even there.

"Quit playin' wit yer dick," one yelled from the back seat. Sy stopped and turned to look without removing his hands from his pockets. "What you lookin' at?" the same one asked.

He continued walking.

"That's right."

Drive away, Sy thought. He begged. *Drive away and leave me alone.*

The truck pulled away, and he let out a deep breath. He turned back one more time to look at the fence. The LOT truck drove right on by it, none the wiser.

***

"So everyone has figured out the food situation?" Sy asked Mateo.

"Yeah, all good. They've been eating."

"I hope they are comfortable enough." He yawned and walked up the steps to Chandra's room, knocking and then poking his head in. She sat on the floor, playing with Sejal, Siva asleep on the bed.

Chandra smiled. Her face glowed, but her cheeks were gaunt and her eyes sunken.

"I ate some yogurt and oatmeal!" Sejal said.

"All right!" Sy said. "You eat with Santiago?"

"Yep!"

"Good." He turned his attention to Chandra. "Have you eaten?"

"Some," she said. "Enough."

Sejal went back to her paper dolls, humming a song. Sy took one last look at Chandra before leaving the room. A skeleton of a woman.

He made his way back down into the common area, where it was empty. He could hear people milling about in their own rooms, but this room stood quiet.

He needed food. He grabbed a portion of thawed waffles and two sticks of string cheese. He wouldn't microwave the waffles even if the electricity was turned on. Hot, soggy waffles were disgusting. He preferred room temperature, soggy waffles. He finished them on the walk to his room, taking his last bite before he even sat down on the edge of his bed. After a brief rumination about whether or not something on his glass window was a bug or a speck of mud, he felt his eyes heavy. He surrendered.

When he awoke, it was dark. The change in day threw him, and he checked the clock in the common room from his doorway as he rubbed his eyes. Seven. *Son of a bitch,* he thought. His headache reminded him that his siesta was more of a sleep. He stretched his chest by clasping his hands behind him and, for the first time, he felt the soreness in his solar plexus from the baton. "Fuck," he muttered and rotated side-to-side at his hips, simultaneously stretching the fascia of his chest. "Reef, you up?"

Reef appeared in his doorway. "You look like shit."

"Can't catch up on sleep, man. What ya reading?"

Reef looked at the book in his hand. "*Slaughterhouse Five.*"

"I can't remember the last time I read that. College?"

"I'll drop it on your bed when I'm done. But that means you gotta actually sit down a little while at a time without falling asleep."

Sy tilted his head. "I have a high motor."

"Or a brain you don't want to listen to," Reef said.

"What are you, a fucking therapist the last few days?"

Reef laughed, and it echoed around the hollow room. "Just calling a spade a spade."

"Bill me."

"I still take Christmas gifts," Reef said. "Size

large." He disappeared into the darkness.

Sy glanced out the window. It was a clear night. Stars littered the sky, innumerable and scattered perfectly imperfect, as if someone had haphazardly punched holes through a backlit canopy. They twinkled out-of-sync in a beautiful concerto of light that made absolute sense, albeit chaotically.

There were no stars like these in Tarrytown, New York. Well, there were, he just couldn't see most of them. He was far enough away from the City to avoid some of the light pollution, but it just wasn't anything like the sky this far out in the middle of nowhere. After two-and-a-half long years, it was one of the only things Sy *wasn't* sick of. Most of the time. Beautiful as they were, they were also a reminder of home—a reminder that he was so far away, in so many ways.

"Seymour?" Priscilla's voice shook him from his thoughts. He turned to see her standing in the doorway, the blanket around her shoulders but a healthy posture about her.

"You look like you're feeling better."

She nodded and smiled. "I just wanted to say thank you. Joseph came by a little while ago and checked in. Changed my bandages again. I'm lucky to have been placed with you all." She looked like she'd been crying.

"He's not going to have any clothes left after shredding all of his," Sy said, smirking. "I'll have to rip some for him for tomorrow."

Priscilla looked concerned.

"I'm joking. And no need to thank me. We all take care of each other. It's just what we do."

"Is it always this quiet after the sun goes down?"

Sy could barely make out her face in the darkness. "Depends. Sometimes people convene in the common room or in someone's bedroom. But sometimes everyone just wants to be alone." He clicked his lamp on and they both squinted, even in its dull light. "Please, sit." He gestured to his bed. She did, gingerly. She was clearly still in pain, both from the wound and her leg. He sat in his wooden chair against the opposite wall.

"I guess this could be worse," she said. "I mean, I've never been to prison, but I've been in close proximity most of my professional life. Sucks nonetheless." She sighed, and with a softer voice, said, "Still, I guess . . . it's no Auschwitz."

"Have you ever been to Auschwitz?"

"When I was twenty."

Sy pursed his lips.

"I went with my family," Priscilla said. "We're not practicing Jews, but my parents thought it was an important trip for me and my sisters to take. Ended up being important for them, too. They gained perspective I don't think they ever had before that. They bickered a lot before the trip. We all did. But the quibbling turned down a few notches after that. And it lasted, surprisingly. It's too bad not everyone has such a sobering experience."

"What do you mean?"

"Just throngs of people taking pictures of themselves and their friends. Too many smiles. Too many . . . I don't know, I'm judging. But it pissed me off. How about you?"

"No."

"It's odd. There, Nazis didn't care about people dying. Hell, they herded them into the gas chambers straight off the train. Worked them to death. Literally. The other inmates would carry their dead back to be buried after the workday. They packed them in like sardines. No one had their own bedroom. They barely had clothes. No heat. No water most of the time. They were fed soup and bread."

Sy was fascinated by how accepting Priscilla seemed to be. Maybe it hadn't hit her yet. Maybe it had, and she was incredible at hiding her fear. Or maybe she was just a strong woman. She was as composed as anyone he'd ever seen arrive just a day before, though shock wasn't out of the question. Through her fever and infection, to the realization of being in her own prison hell.

"Because they don't necessarily want us to die," he said. "Granted, I don't think they care much if we do, but that's not the point of this. They aren't tricking us to simply put us into a gas chamber. They want to convert us. Brainwash us. Mentally beat us into submission. Physically, too." Sy pushed his hair off his face. "If we don't die, they let us sit here 'til we decide we've had enough and have 'woken up.'" Then you can volunteer for—"

"The SLRs," she interrupted.

"Exactly. How do you know about them?"

"That's all they talk about out there. And then once you get to the warehouse, people share all the information they know. But the LOTs do a good job suppressing it. All I know is, if you don't get through the seven interviews—interrogations—they shoot you in the back of your head and burn your body. They don't feel it's worth it to put you back into camp and try again. But that's the part they try to keep hush-hush."

Sy swallowed hard.

"If you pass the SLRs, your life is forever damned anyway," she continued. "They brand a fucking L on the inside of your wrist, like a Scarlet Letter. Then you wear an ankle bracelet until the next election. Your vote proves you're an asset to society. You work shitty, menial jobs and get paid whatever they decide minimum wage is at that time. Nothing's set. After all that, you're allowed back into public as a normal citizen. But you're monitored. They check your voting record. They check your internet activity. Social media. Phone calls. Everything."

"So things have progressed," Sy mused.

"It's become the world now," she said. "Spreading everywhere, like a plague. Even picked up some steam overseas, apparently. But it's all rumor. No one really gets concrete information anymore.

The internet is completely neutered. Television might as well not exist."

"What happens if there's a rebellion and they're voted out?"

Priscilla smirked. "No one's on the ballot that they don't want on the ballot. Only dummy selections for monitoring and purity. The dummy selections even faux-campaign. Hired actors."

Sy's heart slowly escaped from its place in his chest and moved to his throat, where he choked on it.

"And there's nothing you can do but wait, pack your sack that they provide for free at any city hall if you don't have one to use, and hope you're forgotten about. But everyone goes eventually."

"Your entire family go at once?"

"My two sisters went first. Then it was my turn just a day later. We ended up in the same warehouse together, somehow. Recognizing them from across the room and weaving through the hordes of people was the happiest I've ever been in my life. It was short-lived, though. They separated us on the train. When I went after them, a guard shouldered me into the car wall, where I bounced off and onto a sharp piece of metal trim around the floor. Only thing I had to hold up against the cut was a shirt from my sack. A kind man held it until I could get into a position to lie on my bag and stop the bleeding." She winced and shifted her body. "It was infected before the day-long ride from Ohio was even over. I knew it because I felt the fever come on about an hour before we got off the train. And then my leg started hurting not long after they shuffled us into the trucks, and I got stepped on. Then someone who had some first-aid gauze in their sack helped bandage my back."

Sy took a deep breath and cleared his throat. "Christ."

"You? How did you get *here*?" she asked, spitting out the word.

"My parents and I had packed our sacks long before then. They didn't really need to. Dad wasn't at risk of being taken away, and Mom never voted. So we weren't sure there. But he wouldn't let her go without him, so he packed. He'd have voluntarily gone had she been detained. We took precautions. Thankfully. New York caved when they could no longer hold the military out. Even most of our police and fire department stepped in to defend us, but it didn't matter. I was sitting at my kitchen table. I managed to compose myself enough to grab the sack I'd packed. They took my phone right away and patted down the sack, but felt it was soft and let me hold onto it. The real check didn't come until the warehouses, where they x-rayed the bags. It was lax up until then. I honestly wondered whether or not it was going to be so bad. Premature on that front."

"Not lax anymore," Priscilla said. "It's much, much stricter since LOT officers were being ambushed at the point of arrest. Some were killed, others maimed."

He leaned the wooden chair back on its hind legs and up against the wall of his room. "They really managed to get some of them?"

"More than some," she said. "It was a real problem. They had to change the way they went about arresting."

"I'd thought about it," said Sy. "I can't lie. But, in the moment, I couldn't believe it was actually happening. You saw it on the news. You heard from people. But you never thought you were going to be one. You did, but you didn't."

Priscilla pushed her own hair out of her face. Clearly, she hadn't thought about how little the older tenants of the world knew about the present-day world outside.

"I thought about my brother a lot, at first," Sy continued, "and how he'd abandoned our family yet was revered as some hero because he served in the military."

"Was he?" Priscilla asked.

"He was involved in the occupation of East Jerusalem. Saved a bunch of his unit by finding an IED before it was detonated. He was a hero to his men, but I guess when is anyone ever a hero to their enemy." He shook his head. "When he got home, people treated him like he walked on water. Hell, even I was impressed. But something as simple as a vote kept him and his family safe. And mine put me here."

"What about your parents?" she asked.

Sy shrugged. "They never blamed him for

moving on with his life, leaving them behind." His throat caught in the emotion of the sentiment. He tried pushing it away like he always did, but with Priscilla staring him in the eyes, he couldn't. Tears forced through, and he covered his eyes and sobbed for a time. He sniffled and looked up. "I worry more about my father than I do my mother. I just hope her being married to a Loyalty Party voter saved the both of them."

"It did," she said. "If a non-voter is married to a voter, they don't take that person away. Only warn them, making sure they vote the right way from then on out."

Sy placed his face in his hands again, overcome with happiness. A foreign feeling. He wasn't sure how to handle it.

"Single non-voters were also warned. Sternly." Her voice seemed more mature than he'd previously noticed.

"How old are you?" Sy asked, blunt.

"Thirty-two."

His eyes widened. "I would've guessed mid-twenties, at most!"

"I've always looked younger. I even tried to lie and tell them I wasn't able to vote at the time and it had to be a mistake. But all my social media ranting and raving before the third term began—mostly me antagonizing 2016 voters—sold me out. We were all too self-absorbed to see what they were doing right under our noses."

Sy ran his hand along the unpainted cinderblock wall and scoffed. "Military training facilities."

"State-of-the-art." She snorted. "What did you do before all of this?"

"I recovered data from defunct and busted hard drives. Dad's business was a paper manufacturing company. Started at the bottom and worked his way to vice president, but I just wasn't interested in managing people. My father is that guy. Not a bad guy, but that's just how he is. Whatever. Old school, you know?"

Priscilla pulled the blanket a little tighter around her shoulders. "My dad's the same way. Both he and Mom are fine, I'm sure. They were in so much denial that when people who had come up missing were found in internment camps, they believed those people would learn something and come home better for it. Like this is summer camp. It's so fucked. I called to tell them a truck had pulled up in front of my apartment and that I loved them. I left a voicemail. My final goodbye. A goddamn voicemail."

There was a brief silence.

"Have you always been so composed?" Sy asked.

"I guess." She wasn't bragging, her tone almost disappointed. "I'm good at internalizing my panic and grief. And then I let it out slowly instead of all at once."

"What did you do?"

"I'm a lawyer. Was a lawyer."

"Wow." He let out a huff of air. "That's impressive as hell."

"Not quite as impressive as it sounds." She shrugged. "The job certainly isn't." She fiddled with the corner of her blanket.

Sy smirked. "Sorry—lawyer is impressive, no matter the circumstance." He paused a tick. A mote of dust fluttered past the light bulb inside the lamp. "I'd love to be a fly on the wall when this history lesson is taught, one day."

"I've read this story too many times," she said. "Before and after. Studied dictatorships and fascists in college. It was interesting. Until it repeated itself."

"And here we are." Sy sat the chair back down on all four legs.

"I always pictured death differently," Priscilla said. "It didn't look like this. It was scarier and not so . . . so . . . *infuriating.*"

"I think death looks different to everyone. Every time. When I first got here, he was ugly and he smelled putrid. And he flashed around like he was teleporting." Sy shook his head, overwhelmed at the thought, all these years later. "Maybe I'd see him on top of the razor wire on the fence. Or in the eyes of a LOT officer. But now?" He looked out of the window. "He looks like that. Like a void. Empty. When you're sure you're going to die, it's clearer, I guess. But it's vague when you're fighting, and you feel in control when you're not at all. The void is faceless. Timeless. Eventually, death kicks in the door. Docs for everyone. But I just refuse to let him in before that. I refuse to give him a face, one iota of thought unless I have to. And maybe not even when I have to." He thought of the fence outside. The SLRs. The Marlons.

Sy and Priscilla's eyes met and connected until she smiled and they both looked away. "You're older than twenty-eight up there." She pointed to his head.

"We all are. I probably look fifty-eight."

"I look like a wet dog with this greasy hair." It was the first time he heard a little Northeast in her voice. She was comfortable.

"It gets used to the grease, eventually. Then it dries out and, believe it or not, it's fine." He leaned forward. "Smell my head."

She backed away.

"Oh, come on. Just smell it."

"This is . . ." She took a sniff. "Not smelly at all, actually."

"Told you. I just rinse it with water frequently. Sometimes every other day. Give it a little soap once or twice a month. The body acclimates. At least I was hoping it did. I wasn't sure if I really stunk and just got used to it. Thanks for being my guinea pig."

"You suck," she said. She had dark hair and an olive complexion but lacked any distinguishing European features. "What's your heritage?"

"Mostly Chechnyan."

"We're neighbors. Russian. Jew. Ish."

"I'm a close-enough-to-Russian atheist. Second-generation. My parents are as American as . . . well, whatever America used to be. Apple pie. Baseball. Fucking tanning beds. Reality shows." She shivered. "And Elvis. Hence the name."

"Well, no shit. Sounds like they're fun people." The silence was palpable, as was the resentment. She feigned a smile. "Well, other than that. I guess it kept them out of here, no?"

"It's cold," she said, brushing off the question.

"The heat hasn't kicked on in a while. I always just bundle up on the bed and wait for it to come on. It should be soon. They won't let the pipes freeze." He ran his finger along the mortar between the cinder blocks. "You should get some more rest anyway. You'll finish sleeping that infection out of your body." He helped her to her feet by supporting her arm. She felt warm. He squinted at her and then offered a hand for her cheek. She leaned in. It was cool. Of course it was. The room was 64 degrees. But her arms were under the blanket. She was shivering because she was tired and cold, he figured. She hissed and limped extra gingerly on her leg as he helped support most of her weight. Once they got to her room, he sat her gently on her bed. She curled up into a ball again. "It was nice talking to you. You're pretty badass."

"And you . . . well, you don't smell," she said,

her eyes closing already.

He laughed quietly and bundled her with both blankets and walked back out into the common room.

"I think you fucking reek," Reef said from his room.

"Me too," Mateo echoed from upstairs.

Sy shook his head. "You're going to wake everyone up, dickheads."

They cackled.

The only sound Sy hadn't heard in quite some time was Siva crying, he realized. Thank heaven for the baby formula.

SIX

CHANDRA'S SCREAMS launched Sy to his feet, out of the bedroom and directly up the steps. Mateo had gotten to her doorway already.

Sy tried blinking away the junk in his eyes, only truly waking up the moment Chandra cried, "He's not breathing! Not moving! He's blue!"

Sy pushed passed Mateo and into the bedroom. Chandra was pacing the floor with the baby over her shoulder, patting furiously, manically at his back. "Easy. Hand him to me," Sy said, gently taking the baby from her arms. Siva was limp as a ragdoll, and Sy felt the baby's neck and head flop to the side under the support of his hand. He placed Siva on his back on the bed as gently as possible. Siva wasn't blue—he was purple and blotchy. From the looks of him, he hadn't been breathing for quite some time.

"Mateo, watch him. *Don't* let her pick him up again."

Before CJ had a chance to answer, Sy sprinted

full speed down the steps, two at a time. He charged through the common room, bursting out the front door and over the sopping wet pavement and grass in his socks. It had dropped below freezing, and sleet pelted him in the face as he hurried to Building 6. He grabbed for the doorknob, but his hand slipped, jamming into the wooden frame, dislocating his thumb immediately. He felt the awkward angle of the digit before he even saw it. He wasted no time switching hands as a loud "Fuck!" roared from his mouth.

"Joseph!" he yelled as he found the doorway. Joseph was just waking. He'd been drinking a glass of water and sitting at the edge of his bed. The urgency in Sy's voice jolted him to his feet and into his shoes. "The baby's dead. He's dead."

"What?"

"Siva. He's fucking purple and cold. He's dead."

"No one is dead until they are warm and dead," he said as he slipped his shoes on. They both ran as fast as they could back to 8 and up the stairs. CJ had arrived, hearing the commotion, and was holding Chandra while Joseph immediately took the baby from the bed. He placed Siva on the floor. Sy watched the color leave the doctor's face, and the contrast between the baby's purple skin and Joseph's alabaster pallor was striking. "Anything?" asked Sy.

"Yes, anything?" Chandra yelled. She paced the room, talking to herself in Hindi.

The doctor placed his ear on the infant's chest and checked his airway by opening the baby's mouth. "Give me some blankets. Anything warm." CJ tore out of the room and returned with some blankets, one of them a safety blanket. Joseph gave the baby a few small breaths by placing his mouth over Siva's mouth and nose. They were more like puffs. Siva's chest rose up and down with each breath. "His airway is clear." Then he started compressions. Two fingers in the center of the baby's chest—gentle, but firm. Back to a few more breaths. "Someone wrap the blankets around him." It was cold in the room, but Joseph's forehead was damp. He pushed back his silver hair, now slicked away from his face, wiped his brow, and pushed his glasses higher up on his nose. "We need to get him warmer," he said between breaths, still compressing. "Rub his arms and legs. Put your skin to his, carefully. Give him heat. Everyone crowd around."

Reef and Mateo were watching from behind CJ. They pushed into the room while Chandra managed to regain her bearings some. CJ took the baby's legs and feet and rubbed them, trying to get the blood flowing. Sy took the baby's arm and did the same, with Mateo on the other side. Sy noticed that the baby's hands were stiff, almost immoveable. And because of his thumb, it hurt to even rub the baby's extremities.

Joseph shook his head for a split second. It was subtle, almost unnoticeable. He continued the

CPR, and it was becoming apparent that blood had pooled inside the baby's body. The left side of Siva's face was colorless, and a gradient of red to blue to purple ended on the right side. And Joseph knew. He continued, but he knew. About five minutes went by before the doctor noticeably slowed the CPR. Eventually, he stopped completely. "He's gone. I'm sorry." Joseph glanced over at Chandra, who still hadn't muttered a word. Sejal sat by her side, crying but watching everything. "He's okay now," Chandra finally said, her voice a mere whisper. "He's not hungry." She rocked.

"What time is it?" asked Sy.

Mateo walked down a few steps and glanced at the clock. "8:35."

Joseph swaddled the infant tightly and then wrapped him in another blanket to cover his face. Attempting to reserve judgment, though the vitriol in his voice was certainly apparent, the doctor asked, "Do you bury the dead in your culture?"

"We cremate them."

Joseph simply shook his head.

"I know we cannot do that here," she continued. "We can bury him."

"Well, I'd get him ready now, because he will begin to smell if he is not kept outside."

"I will take some time with my daughter. You can leave us, please."

Joseph turned and left the room without a word.

The gathering cleared, with Sy the last to leave. He turned at the doorway and looked to the bundle on the cold, concrete floor.

I thought we'd make it.

***

The chill was replaced by heat blowing through the vents, upon which old cobwebs and dust fluttered. Sy headed for his bedroom, but a murmuring from Priscilla's room caught his ear. He poked his head in. Joseph was leaning over the woman, examining her back. "All good?" Sy asked.

"Her fever is back," Joseph said. "She's on fire again. I'm going to change her bandage and head back to my building to get more antibiotics."

Sy entered the room and looked down at Priscilla, whose glassy eyes looked like they burned horribly. Joseph was right, naturally. She was giving off heat, even as she shivered. "Nice while it lasted," she muttered, laughing pathetically.

"Did you wake up like this?"

"Thinking back, I started feeling it as we were talking last night, but just thought I was tired. Not so much." She blinked longer than normal. "What was all the commotion?"

"Nothing," Sy said, forcing a smile and cradling his injured hand. "One of the kids fell down. Joseph was checking on him. He's fine."

"Oh. good."

Joseph stood and nodded to the door.

"I'll be right back," Sy said, looking down at tiny Priscilla, her head poking out from under layers and layers of clothes and blankets.

As they walked between buildings, Joseph grabbed Sy's hand, gripped the tip of his crooked thumb firmly with one hand and lower down the thumb with the other. He took a breath and suggested Sy do the same. He stuffed the bottom of Sy's shirt into Sy's mouth to bite down on. Joseph pulled. He worked the joint until it finally fell into place. Sy stopped groaning a few seconds later.

"Keep that as stable as possible for a while. Grab some snow, and ice it tonight and tomorrow. It'll swell, but it won't take long to get back to normal."

"What's going on with Priscilla?" Sy asked through gritted teeth and the burning ache in his hand.

"It's a terrible staph infection," Joseph said. "Something resistant to what I've already given her. It's come back with a vengeance. And I think that's what's going on with her leg. I don't think it has anything to do with her being stepped on. It's inflamed and red where it hurts. I think it's gotten into her bloodstream." He paused. "She's in rough shape, Sy."

"Antibiotic-resistant?"

"Yes."

"So, MRSA?"

Joseph shrugged. "No idea. It doesn't really matter. We have to use what we have."

"Is whatever else you have likely to work?"

"There's no way to tell until we try. I don't have a great feeling about it. It's angry, whatever it is. Eating her up. And these things, septicemia, work fast." They entered Building 6. "I gave her the little bit of Bactrim I had left, which is typically the first thing we try. But when it comes roaring back, it's not good. I have tetracycline, but not the full dose."

"What's the full dose?"

"Three weeks.

"How much do you have?"

"Half. Maybe less. It's only what I've collected over time. I tried to build a full dosage, considering the high likelihood of something like this popping up here, but the medication is scarce and very hard to get. I'm surprised we haven't had to use it in the past. We can administer it, hope it does the trick, and request more from the LOTs. Maybe a week will be enough time to get what we need from them."

"The last time anything got here in time," Sy said, "it was because one of the troopers snuck it in to us. And we still don't have a clue who it was."

"It's the only hope we have. I'll flag the troopers down this time. I'm not so sure they'll be so receptive to you after the other day."

"Or ever." Sy rubbed his chest.

"I'll request linezolid too. Last resort. No harm, no foul. Whatever we get, we get."

"You want me to give her the first dose of the . . ."

"Tetracycline. Yes. I'll give you the medication. Can you remember to administer it every morning and evening?"

Sy nodded.

"I'll be there to check often." Joseph paused. "You doing okay?"

"No." He rubbed his temples and took a deep breath. "How do you do this?"

"Great professors, dedicated colleagues, and repetition."

"It gets easier?"

"It gets statistical. Becomes a percentage. If your batting average is high, you take pride in it and strive for better. Sometimes you get hit by a pitch, or someone throws you a junk ball and fucks you up. But you get back to the plate. There's *always* a next time. But if you can't get your swing back, you'll ruin that next time . . . that next life."

"I just don't think that's how it is here," said Sy.

"Sure it is. The batting average is lower. It's a different level of pitching. But you can still step up to the plate whenever you're due up." He handed Sy a bottle of pills. "One in the morning. One in the evening. Give them to her with milk if you can." Joseph turned and plopped onto the wooden chair, which he'd moved under the window and apparently used as both a reading chair and a nightstand. "Get something to eat, will ya? You're worn."

"You do the same." As Sy trudged to the front door, he was certain he heard a sob from Joseph's room. He stopped to listen, but there was only the silence of the building.

Priscilla was asleep, tight in a ball. The heat was on and the thermometer read 69. Far from freezing. Just about comfortable. He moved closer to her, holding his hand near her face. He could feel the heat radiating from her skin before he touched her.

"Priscilla," he said in a whisper, making her stir in her bed. "Priscilla, you need to take another pill." He opened the bottle on her wooden chair and dumped an orange-and-yellow pill into his palm. Then he filled her cup with a carton of milk from the refrigerator in the common room, careful not to let too much cool air escape. He returned and pushed the pill to her lips. She opened her eyes, not fully awake.

"Here you go, hon. Take this. It's going to help you."

She nodded and smiled deliriously, curling her mouth at the corners into a perturbing grimace-smirk. For some reason, it raised Sy's hackles. She pushed up onto an elbow and took the pill with a small sip of the milk. "Thank you," she mumbled as she closed her eyes again. There was no color whatsoever in her face—it was completely pallid, and her eyelids were nearly translucent. The woman *looked* like a fever.

"Rest until this passes." He pulled the blanket up a bit higher over her shoulder, then left the room.

Back outside, Sy could count the steps of the entire perimeter of all four buildings in this Limbo. He could navigate the property in the pitch black. He could recite how many panels of fence there were and who lived in any window in any building. But other than the Limbos in the distance, he didn't have any real, concrete facts about anything outside of the fence, just ideas and conjecture. The only truth he knew was how far his eye could see of the landscape—a long stretch of absolutely nothing with rocks and boulders and mountains in the distance. The mountains that made up the northern horizon of the camp were covered at their peaks with pure, white snow that barely ever fully melted, even in the heart of summer.

How different was it, truly, from the life he lived before? It was relative. If this small plot of land was the only land he stepped foot upon for years, how did that differ from the plot of land he lived on before his arrest? His apartment, his job, his parents' house, the grocery store, the gym, and so on. Wherever that perimeter ended was as far out as he ever went. Regardless of how large the swathe of land was, did he know what was immediately beyond the farthest of his own personal limits? Does anyone? The greatest scientists, astronomers, and astronauts couldn't tell you what's beyond what they know and where they've been.

Institutionalized. He was, he thought, sure. But everyone is. Aren't they? Silly thought. People have the option of pushing beyond their limits and boundaries, even incrementally, over time. Long periods of time. But that doesn't negate the fact that even when we're venturing farther, we will still always have an invisible perimeter, a fence, that contains our life.

So this was Sy's. This was Reef's. This was Joseph's. For now. Forever, maybe. But it was no different than real life. It was no more limiting than simply going to work.

Institutionalized.

A dangerous thought that he tried shaking away along with the pain in his hand.

He strolled to the side of the property where he had stomped free the rung. He checked to make sure it was where it belonged. Secure.

And when the LOTs drove by a few hours later, he nodded to them cordially. They only stared and scoffed to one another. Though the one in the backseat stared blankly at him, and he could swear he noticed a nod back. *Ah, hello, fellow human.*

When he got back to his building, the low sun was casting the shadows of everything around them down upon their patch of land, Chandra was outside, wrapped in a shawl and barely anything else. In her arms was Siva. Sejal was not with them, and Sy was thankful for that.

She softly recited a prayer in Hindi as she

lowered Siva's body into a cardboard box, which was nested into a slightly larger box. She closed the top, stood for a moment, wiped her eyes, and went back inside, never noticing Sy standing only a few dozen feet away. He walked up to the box and tucked the flaps inside each other until they were locked together. Behind the building were the remnants of a folding wooden chair from one of the rooms in Building 5. It had been broken during a fight a year or so back when a woman named Natalia was fed up with another tenant and threw the not-so-light chair directly at his upper half. It missed and crashed into the cinder wall, splintering into a few pieces and startling the entirety of the building. CJ was present, and stepped in between the two of them, only to get clawed in the face and neck by the infuriated Natalia, reaching for her target, Marcus. Turns out he *thought* he'd gotten a signal from her to make the first move—and by first move, he meant caressing her ass while she walked by him in the common room.

She hadn't taken kindly to the advance and, once the situation calmed, took her opportunity to punch the ever-living shit out of Marcus. He had a shiner, bloody nose, and swollen ear. Not long after the SLRs began, both Natalia and Marcus were some of the first to sign up.

Sy took the sharpest chair leg and walked around to the front. He scanned the property and chose an area near the western fence, where he had just come from. It was a bit more peaceful and secluded than the rest, in the shadow of Building 5. Shrubs and large bushes outside the fence pushed it inward. In other words, it was out of the eyes of the cameras, close to where his loosened rung was.

The temperature plummeted as the sun dipped lower, finally starting to tuck behind the horizon. Sy poked a bit at the dirt and dead grass. It was hard from the freezing temperatures. He opened his stance some and stabbed down as hard as he could, dislodging a clump of dirt. He kicked it away and did the same thing again. This time, the timber shot several splinters into his bare hands, some into his formerly dislocated thumb. He yelped and dropped the chair leg to the ground. He looked down at his boots and bent to untie them. He removed both, took off his socks, and put his boots back on. Then he slid his hands inside the socks and pulled them up his arm.

He grabbed the piece of wood again, and after a few more plunges, enough of a hole had started for him to begin scraping. He scraped with the piece of wood for three hours, into the pitch black and freezing cold, though sweating as he worked. He used the stick, his hands, his boots, until eventually he had enough of a hole to fit the entire cardboard box with a good two or three feet above it. He eyeballed the size but was certain it would drop down deep enough to cover it with a significant amount of dirt. Then he'd mix the dirt with some water and tamp it down tight on top of the box, hoping it would freeze and prevent wildlife from digging it up. He couldn't be certain, but there wasn't much else of a choice. He wasn't going to leave the infant dead and frozen in a cardboard food box. And he'd exhausted his hands beyond the ability to dig any further. The splinters and blisters prevented him from gripping the stick even one more time.

When he appeared in her doorway, Chandra was standing at her window. He could hear Sejal playing with Santiago from his parents' room.

"Those stars never fail to amaze me," Sy said. "I stare at them for hours, sometimes."

"They are so clear," she responded solemnly and without turning to face him. "Siva is with them now, in the stars. And he will come back as someone else. Someone lucky enough to have a good life, not born into horror." She bowed her head.

Is there even a good life, anymore? he wondered.

"It makes me sad, because I think he was in a hard life before this one," she continued. "He always seemed in pain, emotionally. He did not smile at us. He did not ever truly relax. But then last night, he fell into such a deep sleep I didn't think anything was wrong. I was just relieved he was asleep, and deeply. I thought the formula was just so heavy that it made him that way. Maybe he had some peace and relaxation before he moved on."

"Did Sejal say goodbye?"

"Yes. I do not think she fully grasped exactly the consequences and finality of it all. Not yet. I thought I would deal with that when it comes. After all, she cried for a little while and then found herself playing and having fun. But the more I think about it, the more I believe she understands this more than I do. Or has processed it more than I have. She's a tough one."

"Tougher than us." He cleared his throat. "Chandra, I, uh, dug a grave for Siva. I'm pretty certain it's big enough to fit the entire box and have enough room to pack a good amount of dirt on top."

"We always cremate our family members. This is hard for me. But it is what needs to be done." She fought through her emotions and kept a stoic face.

"I would help you in a heartbeat, you know that. We just can't light a fire on the property, unless we want the LOTs coming in and . . ." He stopped as Chandra turned to face him.

"I know this. I was just sharing our culture with you."

"Of course," he said. "I'm sorry. Would you like to be the person to place him in the grave?"

"It's all right, you can do it. But I would like to help you cover it with the dirt. I would like to pray over it and the earth to pass him on to another life. One with lots of happiness and no pain."

She cried, finally. First, she sobbed quietly, and then she cried harder, collapsing into Sy's arms. He held her tightly as she trembled. They both sat down on the bed, embracing. "I'll make sure he is nice and secure in there. And I'll watch it as often as possible. I have a view of it from my room window. You have my word that I will keep my eye on Siva for as long as we're here."

Chandra continued to cry into his chest, and he held her tightly. He had judged her harshly throughout, wondering how a mother could be so clueless as to let her child, her baby, die in the way Siva had. To refuse the food given to her, even though it was affecting her ability to feed him. To refuse the formula at first that may have saved his life if administered earlier. But if he judged her in that vein, he'd need to judge everyone, himself included. Chandra had loved her son. Sy could feel it in her embrace. She did what she thought was the right thing, however she justified it to herself. And, at the end of the day, she was correct—he was simply born into horror.

SEVEN

WHEN SY awoke, he found Sejal on the bed, curled up in a ball next to her mother, a blanket pulled over her. He was leaning up against the wall at an awkward angle. When he shifted his weight to stand, Sejal startled and moved her head onto the pillow with her mother.

The room was cold. Very cold. He bundled the two of them with whatever blankets were around and then blew into his hands. He'd been wearing the same outfit for going on two days and had started to ripen.

He found the communal basin at the back of the common room and brought it into his room. It was still damp from another recent bather.

It wasn't easy to wash in Limbo. Sy would warm the basin by lying under a blanket with it for a period of time. Then he'd microwave a few cups or jars of water and pour them into it. They'd go cold quickly, so he would have to act fast, soaping with "monthly" LOT-issued soap, and then rinsing himself with gusto. Regardless of how hot the water was, by the time it made the trip into the bedroom, hit the basin, and then finally touched his cold skin, he was fighting a losing battle.

It was never pleasant to bathe in the winter, no matter what he did to stave off hypothermia. After rinsing himself as well as he could, he'd quickly jump into bed and dry himself with the dirty laundry and blanket. When he stopped chattering, he would put on his clean clothes and wash the older, dirty clothes in the basin with fresh water. Finally, he'd hang everything from the window ledge using rocks as weights. They'd eventually dry as the heat turned on and off, but it would sometimes take days.

This particular night, the wind made it intolerable outside and nearly as bad inside, had the heat not fought valiantly (when it was on). Drafts whipped through the building. These were the nights the elderly, the very young children, and the frail wouldn't fare well as it got into the morning hours, especially if the heat turned off at an unfavorable time. It was also why there weren't many of those groups currently, save for Alma, tenacious as she was. Everyone, no matter how tough of an exterior displayed, looked forward to that simple little click. The notification that hot air was about to blow through the small vent in every room.

"Why not just override the furnace yourself?" an intro had asked when Sy was an intro himself.

He'd had the same question and was happy not to ask it, risking looking like an idiot. But no one laughed at the man. No one thought the question was ridiculous, at all.

"We don't have access to any underground rooms where the furnace might be," Marcus had said. "We've heard the LOTS built tunnels under everything so they can move in and out without us knowing. And we don't have a clue where any of these tunnels are, never mind the furnace. So digging isn't really an option. Even if we did, when a LOT comes through randomly and finds that we've renovated the place, it won't matter much that the heat works at our command. Not to mention, they'd know within the month that we were fucking with it. It'd be pretty obvious when the usage shoots up significantly. I'd imagine they'd come in here and burn us all at the stake."

But Sy, in fact, had discovered where one of the tunnels was when a local was sneaking them some supplies one summer. "Eastern side of the fence," the nameless man had said. "About thirty yards beyond that hill. You can't see it until you have some elevation. And there's another one on the other side of the compound, where the fourth set of buildings are. I'm guessing it goes straight underneath and out the other side. Imagine they zigzag under all the other Limbos too. Probably has the furnace, storage, offices. It's where the trucks and vans sometimes come from when doing their rounds. Bet it's where they watch y'all from, too."

Sy's ears perked. They certainly seemed to get to the Limbo's quickly when they needed to. Like the first time the tenants had built a bonfire on site, and they were there within minutes to discipline those who were in charge of it. Long before Sy or Reef or CJ or Joseph, in the very early days, there'd been a riot between Building 7 and Building 6. The brawl spilled out onto the grounds, and one man strangled another to death mere seconds before the LOTs made their way through and put a few bullets into the remaining two or three tenants who were involved.

All over some food.

And if they were beneath the Limbos the entire time, regulating the heat, turning off the electricity, surveying every move the tenants made, they'd be even harder to subvert, Sy thought.

The young informant's name was John McLemore, and he was a Wyoming native. He lived about four miles away and would ride his dirt bike to the Limbos, his backpack filled with food and other supplies the tenants could use. It lasted about three months before the LOTs ambushed him on the other side of the fence. He'd thought he'd known the blind spots in the cameras. He hadn't, as it turned out.

"But I voted for him!" John yelled before one of the troopers told him to "eat shit" and shot him in the chest twice while a second trooper, Em, tried to intervene to no avail. Then they ransacked the buildings on the entire compound, taking anything they thought was contraband, anything that didn't align with what they had supplied themselves.

Only a few of the supplies survived, as some of the tenants had been smart enough to hide them on short notice. Thankfully, most of those were linens, providing some extra warmth, and not enough to trigger confiscation.

Sy now wrapped himself in one of those blankets and finally got his temperature back up to simply cold, instead of dangerous. Ideally, they'd all heat endless supplies of water and hover around the steam if they weren't afraid of blowing their only microwave. It had been working for just about five years and would likely be hell to get replaced were it to break.

Sy peeked at the clock next to the thermometer in the common room. Just beyond midnight. Every real sleep was always a long sleep. That was the thing in Limbo. When you *actually* slept, you slept deeply. Because Limbo itself was restless, that meant good sleep was hard to come by. The elements sometimes made it nearly unbearable to even think, never mind slumber peacefully. The internal clock and periodic lack of electricity. The constant disturbances throughout the buildings. Worrying about food. Worrying about sickness and disease. Worrying about heat. Worrying about sanity. No, Limbo didn't *want* you to sleep.

So when you crashed, you crashed hard. They called it the *Limbo coma*. The subconscious mind was trained to be prepared, and that made it even harder to get into that deep sleep everyone desired. A few months of Limbo and the slightest hum of a truck or van or automobile of any kind propelled you from your bed like a pilot ejecting from an aircraft. Unless, of course, you managed a Limbo coma. And if you asked any of the tenants, they'd take the coma over being always alert.

Before trying it himself, Sy made his way to pay a visit to Priscilla. He'd hoped the cold would keep the fever down without ibuprofen or acetaminophen available. Before leaving her room the last time, he'd placed a cool cloth on her forehead, which he now removed as a warm compress from her sleeping body. She hadn't moved much. When he pulled it away, though, she stirred. She didn't seem much worse than earlier, but he noticed that her skin was clammy.

"How you feeling?" he asked gently.

She moved again and said something unintelligible.

"Priscilla?"

She opened her eyes slightly, and they were bloodshot and glassy.

"My legs. They hurt," she mumbled.

"The same leg?"

"Both," she managed.

She'd been in the same position for hours on end and was likely cramped. "Let me move you," he said. He put his arms under her body and shifted her

117

on the bed. She moaned pathetically, as if every nerve was exposed.

"My neck."

"Stiff?"

"Yes. And it hurts . . . even if I don't . . . move."

He soaked the cloth in the sink again and draped it over her forehead. Her face contorted. It did not feel good, he knew, but it was necessary. "It takes time for the antibiotics to work. I'm sure it'll break again. Go back to sleep and try to relax. You'll feel better by morning."

Again, she mumbled something unintelligible.

"What's that?"

"Lie with me. Warm."

The heat was still in fuck-you mode. Sy went back to his room and collected the two blankets he'd been using. When he returned, he made her lift her head and sip some cool water. Then he shifted her over again. She moaned worse this time. She smelled—a combination of sour skin and something else he couldn't quite put his finger on. The poor thing hadn't had the opportunity to clean herself since she had been snatched from her home days and days ago. And now she'd been under blankets, stewing in her own body and its infection and all the fluids and smells that came with that.

He climbed under the covers with her and then tossed a few more blankets on top of them both. She was on fire, but his warmth still caused her to press her body up against his. He wrapped himself around her, passing on his body heat. If she deserved anything, it was to be comfortable. "Sweat it out." That's what Mom had always said. Except he knew from Joseph to keep the room cool and dress lightly. Fever 101 for a doctor. Logically, raising the temperature and burning the infection out seemed like common sense. But that was wrong, as Joseph had explained. But she needed his warmth to simply keep a normal temperature around her.

For nearly an hour, she shifted subtly and moaned frequently. Her hand would reach for her neck, and words like "My head aches" would be audible between patches of gibberish. At one point, he noticed a tear from one eye trickle down her cheek. He was sure it was from her eyes burning, until he heard the whimper. The same whimper he'd heard previously. That was also when he heard the click and the whoosh of warm air blast out of the register in her bedroom. A few deep breaths released some of the stress in his body. He tossed a few of the blankets off, nervous of her temperature reaching dangerous levels. *Everyone else will sleep well now, at least*, he thought, relieved. It would be the last thing he would think before fading out of consciousness.

When his eyes fluttered open, it was morning. The Limbo coma. He remained in the same position in which he had fallen asleep and was stiff. At first, he didn't understand what had woken him. It wasn't a natural awakening, but after a second or two, he gained his bearings. Priscilla was cold. She didn't say it. She didn't move. She just was. The coldness could be felt through her clothes and through his. So could the stiffness of her arm as he took his own off hers.

He stared at her. The side of her face was white, as were her hands. Her fingernail polish, jungle green, had chipped away so much that it barely existed. She had been clutching her shawl against her body and the rigor mortis made her clutch it tighter still.

Sy pushed her hair off her forehead and out of her face. He placed a hand on her cheek for a moment, then raised himself from the bed. He pulled the blanket up and over her head.

His breath came from deep within his diaphragm. As he exhaled, he pinched his eyes shut. "I don't pray much," he whispered. He sat on the wooden chair. "Never really did. Not even sure I know how to, anymore. I don't know how the hell someone, something, whatever you are, could allow this." He opened his eyes and stared at Priscilla. "You had so much more to say and do. Instead, you'll only leave this room to go in the ground with the rest of them. The rest of them." He raised his voice a decibel. "And your sisters probably won't make it out alive, either. Neither will I. It's a game of lasting now, isn't it? You told me yourself—no one makes it back here. Not if they escape. Not if they fail their interviews. Never. You walk out those gates and fuck it up, you're dead. But if you stay, you're dead. So we're just . . . dead. What's the fuckin point?"

His brain rattled on. Just a microcosm of life in the Loyalist Party's America, he felt. Cruel and unusual punishment is a manifestation of anything in power, regardless. It's just the natural way. Maybe we aren't capable of anything else. Maybe the advances we seem to make as a species over the years are just a mirage. A one-step-forward, one-step-back game, forever. Running on a treadmill the entire time, regardless of technology, advancements, or modernity. Dancing in place.

He stared at the figure under the blanket for a little while before he stood. "So maybe we're all born at the wrong time." He remembered thinking about how miserable life would've been before modern healthcare, vaccines, disease eradication, antibiotics. And they probably thought how miserable it must've been to be without shelter, farming, food on their tables. And so on. And the ones that come after will think of how miserable this time was for everyone. He swallowed. "I'm sorry I couldn't help you, Priscilla." He turned to fetch Joseph and instead found Reef standing in the doorway. It was hard to make eye contact. Reef hugged him, and he hugged the man back. Then he began crying into Reef's shoulder. "I can't do this anymore," he said, muffled.

"Yes, you can," Reef said. "You can."

"I can't."

"You *can*. Because we have to." He stood Sy back and looked him in the eyes. "If we can, we do. If we can't"—he cast his eyes at the body—"then we don't. But while we're here, we *can*. Because it's what we do. We fight. And if I can, you can. I promise."

"What time is it?" Sy asked, fighting the tears.

Reef peered out of the doorway and looked at the clock. "7:05."

"I need to get Joe. Then I need to dig another plot."

"It's bitter outside," Reef protested, following Sy to his room.

Sy put another shirt on over the thermal he already wore. He slipped his boots on and then pulled on his beaten-up coat. "It's fucking bitter in here." He strode through the common room and out the front door.

It had snowed overnight, leaving an inch-thick layer on everything, including the box that held Siva. When Sy realized he hadn't moved the baby last night, he began to crumble inside. The box had lost its rigidity in the wet snow, but nothing had happened to the boy's body, and that was all that mattered. When he tucked it under his arm, it folded and caved. He marched to the grave he'd already dug. He tried to place it inside—the depth was right, but the width certainly wasn't. A solid three feet of space would've been above the box had the crater not been dug inadvertently in the shape of a wedge, hard to tell in the dark the night before. He turned and brought Siva back to the front of the building and fought not to punch the concrete wall in front of him. Instead, he just yelled something unintelligible.

Joseph was sleeping when Sy entered through the common room of Building 6 and peered around the doorway. He must've felt himself being watched and turned to Sy, who was as white as the snow outside.

"Sy?" Joseph asked. "What's up?"

"She's gone." Sy placed the bottle of antibiotics on the back of Joseph's sink. "Save these for someone who might need them."

"How do you know?" Joseph asked.

"She's fucking stiff, ice cold, shit and pissed herself. Dead."

Joseph stood from his bed, his eyes locked on Sy. He slipped his shoes on. "Let's go see her."

"I have to bury Siva."

"Can Reef or Mateo help?"

"No."

"I'll help, then."

"Do what you need to for Priscilla. I'll take care of Siva. Thank you, though."

And Sy did, burying the infant's box with the frozen remnants of dirt that he managed to break up with the chair leg and his boots, and removed handful by handful.

When he was done, he brought Chandra and Sejal outside to help with the burial. He needed water to mix with the dry, winter dirt, so he returned to the building to retrieve the basin. He filled it halfway with water and returned outside, pouring it over the soil.

He used the broken chair leg to stir it all up some and tamped it with his boots, careful not to apply too much weight that would crush the box below. *Not that it matters. He'll decompose in weeks anyway.* He then left Chandra and Sejal to their family, taking a long stare at Sejal as he walked passed her. "Are you okay?" he asked the little girl, who didn't seem so little in the moment. She didn't answer. Didn't have to. He nodded to Chandra and continued on inside.

The building felt warm when he walked through the common room. It always did when coming in from outdoors. He walked passed Priscilla's room, where Joseph and Reef were by her bedside, and entered his own room. He shook off his coat and snatched a rubber band from the window ledge, tying his hair atop his head. He chugged a cold cup of water and then filled it a second time, drinking half. He leaned up against the wall, his head connecting with the concrete with some force. It didn't faze him.

He could hear the others talking. The entire building was awake. Sejal was now at the front door, calling her mother. Mateo sat at the top of the steps, avoiding the sight of the dead body and the fetid stench she'd emitted. Reef spoke to the doctor. "I came over when I heard Sy talking. Woke me up. Goddamn brutal few days."

"Sy's taking it rough," Joseph said. "It's like it's been following him lately."

"I felt her. It woke me up," said Sy, as he

made his way to the room. The doctor flinched, unexpectant. "I fell asleep with her, trying to warm her up. She asked me to. Tried using my body heat." He gestured to Priscilla. "Didn't work."

"She's been dead for hours," Joseph assured him. Something seemed to hold him back.

"It's okay. Keep going."

"Her legs are nearly twice the size they should be. She had a horrible infection throughout her entire body. She was septic, likely had meningitis, and there was *nothing* you could have done to save her. Nothing any of us could have done, besides what we did. You comforted her in the final hours of her life and she died with someone beside her."

"What if it was MRSA?" Sy asked.

"We can clean the room from top to bottom," Joseph said. "We've got a small bottle of bleach about a quarter full. If we dilute it, we should be able to stretch it out enough to clean the entire room. We'll toss the linens and anything else disposable into the shit trench."

Sy looked at the bed, then stripped off all his clothes. He tossed everything onto the bed next to Priscilla's body. "We'll wrap her in a blanket and burn her body."

Reef turned to him, his head tilted in concern.

"We have to."

Reef helped Sy carry Priscilla's body, wrapped in blankets, along with Sy's clothes, to the trenches.

"Are you sure—"

"We have to burn her in the trench," Sy interrupted. "I don't want to risk leaving anything behind."

Reef stared ahead as they walked across the yard.

"And the smoke won't be as visible."

"What if the entire trench goes up?"

"It's too wet." Sy was short and blunt. He didn't want to talk. He didn't want to think. He didn't want to *be* right now. "And if it does, so be it."

After briefly placing Priscilla's body on the ground to take the matches from his pocket, he struck one against the pad on the back of the plain white cardboard. The top and bottom of the blanket had been soaked in some of the small amount of hand sanitizer Building 6 had on hand. The rest was distributed on Priscilla's body and clothes. The blanket ignited slowly as Sy held the match to the foot-end of Priscilla's death shroud. The dry, windless day helped. After igniting the top half and waiting for it to catch, Sy and Reef quickly picked up the bundle, got down as low as they could, and dropped Priscilla's body onto the piles of excrement. The blankets opened on impact, a flap of fabric unwrapping to display Priscilla's hand and arm.

Reef looked away. Sy stared. He stared until the rest of the blanket ignited. Until Priscilla's body became an inferno. Until her hand and arm turned black, eventually to carbon. Reef backed off, but Sy kept vigil. He stood over the funeral pyre until the flames extinguished and a heap of soot and charred body was all that was left. Then the two of them sprinkled whatever was left of the wood chips over the remains, covering Priscilla.

"Are you okay?" Reef asked. Sy walked away without answer, making a beeline somewhere ahead of him, to the area of fence he'd begun loosening. He pushed past the dormant bushes and grabbed the rungs and began kicking at the lower part. He kicked and stomped and pushed. He pulled and shoved with his hands until his fingers bled. Tears streamed down his cheeks. He turned and slammed his back to the fence. "Let me the fuck out of here!" he yelled, a guttural growl.

CJ started toward him from where he stood, in front of Building 8, but Reef held him back. Sy stared at them, then walked a few feet farther and turned his attention to the security camera mounted on the pole, along with the speakers. "Let me the fuck out of here! I know you can hear me. I know you can see me. I know you can always hear and see us. So help me, if you don't let me the fuck out of here, I will let myself out, goddamnit!"

Finally, Reef approached him. He grabbed Sy around the shoulders and walked him back to the front of the building as the blood dripped down his hands, down his fingers, and dribbled to the hardened dirt.

EIGHT

MAY IS near perfection in almost any of the top half of the continental states. The blooms on the trees are intact early on and start to spit off a week or so in, displaying the beautiful leaves underneath, leaves that change colors throughout the months, only to die again when the cold strikes. But who cares? That's later. Much later, so it feels. So everyone hopes. Contrasting the reds and oranges of fall, the whites and yellows and purples of spring are exploding with life. Hopeful. It's like the day before a vacation, all ahead of you. The warm weather, the break from the bitter, and the guarantee that you wouldn't freeze to death on any given night.

In Wyoming, however, it's a half-step from heaven. The temperatures are perfect. The air feels clean and purified. And when you've survived another winter in Limbo, it's nirvana.

The annuals and perennials bloom even within the confinement of the property, as pollen and seeds propagate by wind and wildlife. Sagebrush and swale infiltrate the land wherever dirt can be found, and in some of the luckier years, mule's ear and Indian paintbrushes bloom from them. The paintbrushes looked exactly as they sounded—dull green stems turning red (or sometimes white or yellow) in a dramatic, brush-shaped gradient. The tenants of the Limbos would pick the flowers and dress their windowsills using whatever they could to prop the elegant flowers upright. The paintbrushes never lasted long once picked, but they were splendid in the meantime.

Sy transferred and planted an already-bloomed bitterroot as the memorial marker for Priscilla. The oblong petals were lavender this year, and because the stems grew no flower, they were striking against the grass around them. It was a few feet from Siva, whose grave was tended mostly by Chandra. That same nook was where most of the bushes flourished, as the sun was shielded by Building 6 for part of the day, which helped to not burn the leaves. The perfect balance of light and dark, forcing the bushes to grow quickly and with vigor. Some even grew from the hillside right on through the fence, erasing the boundary where Limbo began and the real world ended. It could've been a portal, where someone might transport right through the fence amongst foliage. That's what Sy pretended sometimes, pressing his body into the leaves and limbs, disappearing for a moment or two.

The bushes also hid the weakest part of the fence, where the welding had started to decay the most. Where, once a week, Sy would stomp a rung until an end popped free. Then he'd replace it and work on the next one in either direction. He'd do it in conjunction with the day's hustle and bustle, disguising the sound in whatever way he was able. People closing doors. Laughs. Coughs.

***

"I was just a kid from the suburbs like the rest of 'em, except I was black. Guess that was scary for some people," Reef said.

"For a lot of people," said Lysha, her voice flat.

"How long you been black?" Sy asked Reef, fighting a laugh.

"Since like, '91. My dad was just tired of things being so damn easy for us. He wanted a challenge."

Lysha choked on her water as a laugh escaped her throat.

"Oh, I get it. You should've seen the Jewfro I had going on in grade school. My mom kept it just long enough so that it didn't fall. It teetered on the *brink* of falling, then she'd trim it just enough to keep it upright."

"Oh, that's definitely the same."

"Man, I looked like Napoleon Dynamite."

"And now you look like Slash," Reef said. "Except he's half black. So, you're like Slash's white side.

"You look like a roided out Bob Marley."

"It has gotten pretty long," Reef agreed, pulling a lock of his hair down past his chin.

"And you know it looks cool," Sy said.

"It's gone soon. I don't think I can stand it through the summer. Sleeping on it is hot and annoying. And itchy, between the hair and the beard." He scratched at his face.

"If we can get some scissors, I can do it for you," Lysha said. She had been a cosmetologist before going back to school for her degree in education and had only been teaching a few months before she was snatched up.

Those who managed to slip through the cracks or evade the LOTs were finally starting to get rounded up as the herd dwindled. People handled the detaining in one of two ways: Either they worried relentlessly and had a hard time living their lives until their number was called, in a constant state of panic and anxiety, self-medicating and ruining themselves before it ever even came to fruition, or they simply went about their lives, and if it happened, it happened. Lysha was the latter. She'd made the switch back to school *after* the detaining began.

She certainly needed no one to stand up for her, but when the squat, female LOT name Lori delivered the slap to her face, it almost cost Sy his life. Lysha cocked back to swing and Sy managed to grab her arm before she delivered the blow. Incorrectly thinking Sy was going to hit the guard, CJ tackled Sy to the ground. Fatty Arbuckle fired off a warning shot, which penetrated and lodged in the cinder of the building. CJ and Reef both pleaded with the trooper that it was a misunderstanding, but it didn't stop the female trooper from punting Sy's face with her steel-toed boot, knocking him out cold for half a minute.

The concussion was brutal. Sunlight made him vomit. Lamplight made him vomit. Darkness made him vomit. A solid week in bed and ibuprofen smuggled in by a new face helping from the outside were the only medicine available. It had to do, and Sy slowly recovered.

Lysha repaid Sy's attempt at standing up for her by keeping him company in his dark room, a blanket hung over the window for as long as he needed. She'd taken Priscilla's bedroom after the bleach had—hopefully—eradicated the remnants of what possibly took her life.

The first thing Sy did was tell Lysha what had happened in there, and he even offered to switch rooms with her if she wasn't comfortable enough. That would have been a big no-no, because assignments on file specified rooms for each tenant. Caught in a different room, you were punished.

"We'd keep our stuff in the assigned rooms

and just switch when an inspection comes in, if that makes you feel better," Sy suggested.

"I'll be fine," Lysha said with a smile. "Don't need protection, sweetheart." She was cocky. Five-foot-three on a good day, petite, her hair always in two tight buns at the top of her head. She wasn't quite dark-skinned, but no one would describe her as light. Mocha fit the bill, and she had brown eyes lit with fire behind them. When she wasn't extending a helping hand around the Limbo, she was doing Sudoku or crossword puzzles from books she'd packed in her sack. She wasn't smart. She was extremely smart.

"What's it like out there now?" Sy had asked when first out of his stupor, as he did with every intro. Outside knowledge was key to remaining motivated and involved. In touch, maybe.

"Dead souls in a dead world. It's as if 1950 threw up on all of us. I've never been called a nigger more in my life. It's part of the lexicon again. Like retard and faggot never truly went away. I guess this didn't either, but there's no more looking around before saying it. Entire families have fled. Canada has taken as many Americans as their system can process, but it's almost impossible to get up there anymore. They're still taking as many as they can, but if you can get to the border, you're pretty much guaranteed arrest by one of ours, if you don't get picked off first. Upstate New York, North Dakota, Montana, everywhere. There are even some residents who live near the border who shoot at people crossing over. There've been Canadian Border Services Agency officers killed in the process. They're risking their lives taking in *American refugees*. Let that soak in."

"And you didn't try to flee?" It wasn't a judgment as much as it was concern.

"My mother was a sixty-four-year-old diabetic on dialysis and in a wheelchair. I couldn't leave her behind, and there was no way she'd make it up there with me. So I took care of her. When she passed, I made up my mind that I wasn't going anywhere. If that meant I ended up here, so be it."

"You had no one to go with you?" Sy wondered.

"Just kind of worked out that way, I guess." She looked at him hard. "I'm no goddamn cliché. I do better on my own. My few close friends were long gone—detained, dead, or in Canada before things really broke down. It was just me."

"I didn't mean anything by . . ."

She shook it off. Sy wished she'd made a run for it.

"So I'll stay here and survive as long as I can until someone stops all of this." She shrugged. "Or I die. That's okay too. So be it. I just hope it's a bullet rather than something long and drawn out."

No one would stop it. No country had the balls to step in for fear of being crippled by both the USA and Russia. Even China had begun to look the other way, according to the new intros. Their economy was tanking, but there was no other way. Most countries had struck deals with the president to allow their exchange students and people on work visas to leave the country. And there was nothing he loved more than purifying the American pool—there was nothing his supporters loved more, either.

Mexicans and anyone from south of there who weren't in camps were wrangled into vans by the dozens and dumped onto the other side of the wall. Some estimated that about half of them were U.S. residents, but their credentials were barely looked at, if at all. Mexico was the closest to conflict the country faced, as they fired at U.S. Border Patrol for crossing country lines to dump human beings in piles on the desert lands. A small firefight had even broken out on US soil, the first battle on American land since World War II.

Within weeks, Lysha's attitude had lifted the spirits of the entire Limbo, though. A spitfire, she kept constant conversation going throughout the complex. She learned everyone's name in days, figured out where they all lived, and made sure to associate with them frequently. If someone were to run for mayor of Limbo 5-8, Lysha fit the bill. She was so damn genuine.

Sy admired her.

Reef laughed. "Bob Marley. You fuck."

"Hey, man, Slash was pretty creative. Half-black, half-Jew. It's like if they slammed the two of us together into one person."

"Maybe if we knew how to play an instrument," Reef said.

The three of them, Sy, Reef, and Lysha, sat along the fence, eating their dinners as they waited for Davey, the smuggler. Their relationship with Davey had come a long way. At first, Sy had refused to let him sneak them so much as a pencil. Not after what had happened to McLemore. But Davey was different. He wasn't from Wyoming. He had been born and raised in Chicago and had voted the *right* way as an eighteen-year-old. He had grown older and formed his own opinions but continued to support the president as a deterrent, as tons of U.S. citizens started doing to keep safe. The president was midway through his third term and had won the last election with 92 percent of the vote. The other 8 percent were assumedly red herrings, set up to make it look like a true democratic process. A landfall victory for the POTUS!

Sy wondered if he would have fallen in line too, given the chance at another election. But he'd stuck to his guns twice. Though that had been before spending years in Limbo 5-8. He didn't know for sure, but he knew he'd be open to it. And that disappointed him.

But Davey was a true rebel. He ran things between Limbos for miles on end. Hundreds of buildings with thousands of people, and that was just in the small concentration of buildings in central

Wyoming. He slept in a small apartment over a garage he rented not too far away and made a living working at the regional LOT headquarters, a half-mile distant. The irony. The cojones.

"Like taking candy from a baby," he said, the confident twenty-something that he was. "It's not dangerous when you understand how they execute. Then they're fucking predictable." He paused for a millisecond. "Most of 'em."

"You're nuttier than a Snickers bar, my man."

Truth was, he wasn't nutty at all. He was brilliant. And perhaps slightly loony.

Instead of being a showoff, he kept a low profile and helped thousands of people. He knew every nook and cranny of every LOT complex. He knew camera angles. He knew the ins and outs of each LOT stronghold in the area. He'd have a statue or two in his likeness one day, if it didn't all come *completely* crashing down, but Sy often wondered *how* he kept such a low profile.

"Easy. I work with these people. They know there's a mole somewhere. Multiple, in fact. A lot more than you'd think. But I keep them thrown off as much as possible."

He worked only after dusk or before dawn. He'd memorized every road in that area of Wyoming, including, and mainly, the dirt paths, and he'd fly around on his dirt bike, spitting fumes as he revved the engine, as did lots of locals in the area. The tenants would hear them ripping through the fields at a distance during any season.

Davey had begun a few years back. The Limbos grew so vast in number that he moved slowly through them, trying to get vital supplies to those who needed them most, spending a few weeks or even months at a time in certain places, seeking out the most desperate of people. That's why it took him so long to get to Limbo 5-8, though he had made a few rounds there years before, when it was first occupied. Of course, it had been a totally different crop of people at that time. And fewer of them.

The area came onto his radar again a few months earlier, once word got around the local Limbos that Priscilla had died of a staph infection due to lack of LOT care and access to proper medication. Drugs—of any kind—were no problem for Davey. Though he never let on his sources, everyone assumed he was friends with a doctor or pharmacist. While controlled pharmaceuticals like opiates and benzodiazepines were easy enough to find on the streets, Davey's came in prescription bottles, with a different name on the label each time. Simple antibiotics, blood pressure medication, insulin, and the like—he was able to access all of it. Most Limbos in the area now had a supply of medication for their tenants, plus extra for any intros brought in, and the rumor was that people were surviving in much greater numbers than before. It didn't alarm the LOTs much, according to Davey, because they just figured people were getting used to living in these conditions. Sy remained skeptical. The LOTs weren't all stupid.

The tenants got creative when it pertained to hiding things. Packing and duct tape from Davey came in handy when storing certain supplies, as inconspicuously as possible, under beds, chairs, sinks and whatever else had a flat surface underneath. The tops of door moldings. Inside window sills.

When Limbo 5-8 was ransacked by LOTs in March, they found absolutely nothing, save for a granola bar wrapper blowing around the camp.

"Must've come from outside the fences," Mateo explained.

"We'll find out," said Fatty. "I'll be sure to check my cameras." He nodded, his mouth curled in a shit-eating grin, like he had just explained aerodynamics. As confident as he was rotund.

Mateo had laughed after the LOT left the premises. "Good luck going through weeks of video, lard-ass."

On this particular trip, as the trio polished off their dinners up against the fence separating them from civilization, Davey was trying to bring the group a somewhat odd request—a case of poker chips with a deck of cards and some dice. It was the doctor's birthday in a week, and there was nothing the man loved more than playing cards. It would be special to him, and he was more than special to everyone in the complex. So a few of the group wanted to give him a small taste of freedom, even if it came at a risk. They knew these trips were saved for emergencies and necessities, but in this particular situation, asking for a gift was fine with them, because they considered showing their gratitude to Joseph a true necessity. Most of them did, anyway.

"Tell me, anyone who opposes this," Sy asked one day in the common room. "I've been hearing rumblings that this should not be something we risk Davey for. I understand that while most of us have spoken at length about this, not every single person was in the know. It might come off as a few of us making a decision without everyone's input, which we typically shy away from doing, right? But with that, I ask, what's it like to have a doctor in here? And such a good one? Do you know what other Limbos would give for our situation? Have you all forgotten what it's like to be without a doctor on site? How about all the people who press their faces up against the fences next door to relay a question to Joseph. How many lives has he saved? The girl next door who walked around with strep for a month before it turned into scarlet fever. What would have happened had it not been for Joseph? You've forgotten the fear."

He waited.

"Let's put the primitive side of our brains away for a minute. Is that too much to ask? For a man who's done as much for us as Joseph has?"

He knew they feared losing Davey and whatever other connections would disappear with him, or so were the worries that got back to Sy and the rest, but most seemed to understand. Most except Ramón. In broken English, he expressed that it was unfair to risk someone's life for the sake of a game, to which Sy responded that it's "unfair to risk the sanity of your fellow humans because of something that isn't important to *you*. But to Joseph, it's just as important as any pill in any one of those bottles." Sy found himself raising his voice. "It's selfish of anyone to deny Joseph a gift for how good he has been to us."

"It is selfish of you to think for everyone," Ramón answered.

"It wasn't just me," Sy snapped. "It was many of us. Reef, CJ, Mateo. People who have been here a long time."

"Oh, that makes it okay, then. Because you have been here longer than I have." He stood up and yelled back. "*Estupido imbécil. Vete a la mierda.*"

Before Sy could open his mouth, Lysha stood as well. "*Cuidado con lo que dices. Si no fuera por Sy, todos estarían muertos.*"

The man looked her up and down, speechless at first. "*Soy un hombre. Puedo hacerme cargo de yo mismo.*"

She scoffed. "*¿A quién le importa si eres hombre? Soy una mujer y puedo cuidarme a mí misma tanto como tú. Más. No eres la mitad del hombre que es. Así que cállate la boca.*"

She turned to Sy. "I think anyone who doesn't understand your point is an asshole." She looked back at Ramón and stalked away.

"Do you think he'll come tonight?" asked Lysha.

"He's never stood us up before," said Reef. "But that sun is getting mighty low."

They couldn't go by the rumbles of bikes in the distance, as there were just too many. The ideal cover . . . and the ideal tease.

"I'm not sure I'll be able to wait until next week to give him the chips," said Sy. "Too damn excited. One of you needs to hold on to the case."

"He deserves it." Reef looked at the changing sky. "How many Limbos have a built-in doctor? A surgeon? It's like, how do you tell the guy that he's not just that—a doctor, a provider. That he's your friend, too."

"I think this is a good start," said Lysha. "Having a group of friends to play cards with. He'll know what we went through to get this."

"He might even curse us out like Santi's father did," said Reef.

Sy chuffed.

"I thought you were going to beat that man's ass right in front of his own son," said Reef.

"I would never," Sy responded.

"I was talking about Lysha."

Lysha shook her head. "I would've waited until Santi went to bed." The three laughed. "That's the last thing we need right now. To fight each other. We've got enough to fight."

The sun dipped lower, and a purple hue took over the orange as if someone had changed a light filter. The crickets began to chirp, and the temperature dipped. But after the winter just past, the cooler air didn't faze any of them in the slightest. Lysha had come in at the tail end of it and experienced a solid month of miserable cold, long enough to already dread the next cold season. She'd voiced her concern multiple times.

"It comes whether we want it or not, unfortunately," Sy had told her. "At least we have real blankets for next year, now. And more safety blankets. None of us will freeze."

Reef agreed. "Time to trash those orange motherfuckers."

Sy cautioned against that. "We'll need them the next time the LOTs blow through the joint. We need to come up with a fire drill. Something that we can change out within minutes."

Their attention turned outside of the Limbo, as the sound of a motorbike in the distance grew closer. "That's him."

"Nah, too far," said Reef.

"That's his bike."

The sound grew louder until a head could be seen above a hill in the distance. Eventually, the rest of Davey appeared, and the dust settled as he parked his bike outside of the fence.

"Gentlemen. Lady."

"Davey, how are you, my friend?" Sy asked.

"Couldn't be better."

"You truly get off on this, don't you?" asked Reef.

"One way I get off. Yeah, I get some kicks. A rush, man. Plus, I love seeing you guys."

"How's everyone in 1-4?"

"Good. Anne rebounded from whatever the hell she had. The drugs helped. She says to give the doctor her thanks and love."

"Will do. Was our request any trouble?"

Davey hung his helmet on the handlebars and reached into the compartment on the back of his bike, where he sifted through a bunch of other supplies he'd brought. He pulled out a metal case. "Chips, cards, and dice. Brand new. Enjoy, my brother."

Sy felt his eyes stinging. Lysha squeezed his arm, and Davey walked through the bush to the area of gate a bit wider in the rungs, meant for the LOTs to feed smaller supplies to the tenants without having to open up the gate. It was just enough of a gap to squeeze most things through one at a time, and oddly wasn't in view of the cameras. When they received goods, they disguised them by taking the long routes back to the building, concealing whatever they had in coats, blankets, boxes, and so on.

Sy met him there and stuck his hand out for Davey's. They shook firmly. "Thank you, my friend. I know this wasn't a normal request. Someday, when I get out of this fucking place, I'm gonna repay you."

"Getting a beer with me is—"

The LOT truck roared up the road out of nowhere, aiming its headlights at the four of them. Sy tossed the silver box deep into a bush. Davey stepped back to his bike as the truck came to a dusty stop ten feet away. He flashed a look at the officers stepping out of the truck, then back to Sy and the rest. His face was different, cold. "Evenin' officers."

The two LOTs, Stretch and Fatty Arbuckle, waltzed slowly to the fence.

"David." Stretch nodded.

"On my way home for a bite, and I see these three out and about."

Fatty had unholstered his pistol. "Stirring up any shit?" he asked, staring down Sy. He ran the barrel of his Glock along the slats of the fence.

Davey chuckled. "Nah. Behaving like good little boys and girls."

"Better be," Stretch said.

"They know better." Davey sneered at Lysha. "Don't ya?"

"Leave her alone," Reef said. "Stop harassing us. Just let us be. We do nothing to you."

Davey narrowed his eyes. "You pollute our land here. You, especially, queer." He moved his attention to Lysha again. "But you, you're a sweet one." He blew her a kiss.

She looked down.

Stretch laughed, as did Fatty. Davey spit on the ground.

"Come on," Fatty said. "You don't wanna get too close to these folk. They're liable to reach out and hurt ya. Don't trust 'em as far as you can throw 'em."

Sy ushered the other two away from the area.

"Where you going, son?" Stretch asked.

"Minding my own business, as I was before. Taking a walk in the nice weather with my friends."

"Friends." Fatty burped out a laugh. "Try not to kill another one of these bitches," he said, staring at Lysha.

Sy could feel the blood boiling to the surface of his skin.

"You're right, David. This one is cute. I'll bet she could take both of us at once."

Lysha opened her mouth to say something, but Reef shushed her.

"Just like that," said Stretch. "Keep that mouth open. Just keep the words out of it before I have to clog it up." He opened the driver's-side door. "Have a good night, now, sweetheart. You too, lady."

"Fucker," Sy said under his breath.

The fat one was opening the driver's side door when he flashed a look at Sy. Had he heard him? He smiled and shook his head. "*Porch monkey*." He laughed. "Mom must be proud, David."

Davey laughed and kick-started his bike. "Night, officers." He peeled away. The other LOTs weren't far behind.

Sy picked up a large, stray branch and lurched at the fence. He swung as hard as he could, and the sound echoed out into the plains. He swung again, roaring as he did. Over and over he swung, until there was nothing left. Then he dove into the bush and pulled out the box. He reappeared, his face scratched from twigs. The clasps had stayed closed, and he stormed off to Building 8, angry at the world, but wildly grateful for Davey.

He clutched the gift tight to his chest.

NINE

"I DON'T know what to say."

Sy looked at Reef and Lysha, both standing in the doorway of the doctor's bedroom. "Hope you enjoy it, and hope you'll have us in to play cards with you. I know there're lots of tenants that are champing at the bit to play. You'll have no lack of regular games."

The doctor, sitting at the edge of his bed, opened the case and admired the clay poker chips inside, along with the deck of cards, dealer chips, and four dice. But the miniature bottle of Jack Daniels was what caught his eye—and stole his breath.

"If anyone deserves a stiff drink in here, it's you, man," said Reef. Sy leaned on the wall, and Lysha sat down on Joseph's wooden chair. "You've more than earned it." He shrugged. "I know it's not great bourbon or anything, and I wish we had some more, but . . ."

"I'll take it," said Joseph, chuckling. Reef

walked out into the common room and grabbed the doctor a paper cup. He handed it to Lysha. She passed it to Joseph, who emptied the little bottle into the cup.

"Happy Birthday, friend," said Sy.

Joseph sipped and closed his eyes. When he opened them again, tears welled, and one made its way free down his cheek.

"Guess we haven't forgotten what it's like to be human, after all," Lysha said.

"No, I'm *sure* I had," said Joseph. "Until that." He took the deck of Bicycle cards from their slot and unwrapped the cellophane, slit the sticker seal, and pulled them from the box. He riffled through them and took a whiff of the pack, then tossed the cards with instructions on them along with the two jokers onto the window ledge, next to where Sy was leaning. He put the deck back in the box, returning it to its slot, and closed the lid. After he latched the clasps, he slid the whole thing under his bed.

"I'll have to figure out a good place to keep it." The doctor drank again from his cup. "Tomorrow. Tonight, I spend my birthday with friends." He held up his cup to Lysha, Reef, and Sy. "Thank you. Once we're out of here, it'll be my turn to treat you all."

"You've treated us already," said Reef. "This is the least we could do.

Lysha looked at the doctor from the wooden chair. "Why'd you become a doctor?" she asked. "It's something I've wondered. Maybe it's the skeptic in me, but it's almost too good to be true that someone as caring and nice as you are would get into the job solely for the purpose of helping people."

"I'm generalizing, but as a young child, you want to become a doctor to help people," Joseph said. "As an adult, you want to become a doctor to make a lot of money. If that child still lives in you, your objective will *always* be to help someone, and the money just becomes the benefit." Joseph sat back on his bed, savoring the small sips of whiskey. "But, admittedly, if you become a doctor with adult intentions, most of the time, you're in it for the money first, helping second. Which is *okay*. That's not saying someone's going to give less of a shit about you. It just means they might not take what was once Medicaid, or they get into the specialties that pay the most, not necessarily that they enjoy the most. So they don't enjoy the work as much, even if they're good at it. And that shows. Lack of bedside manner. Abrupt visits. But it can certainly be both. And for me, I can't say the money wasn't an important factor. Especially what I spent on going to school."

"My student loans still kill me," Lysha said, her chair creaking as she shifted. "Killed, at least. I can't imagine yours."

"And I didn't go to medical school until I was in my thirties. So you're talking just shy of twenty years ago. Not thirty or forty, if I'd gone right out of college, which might have made a bigger difference.

Nothing astronomical, but a bit less."

The sun had just about set, leaving them all in silhouette. Reef grabbed himself a chair from the common room.

"Why so late?" Sy asked.

"I was in the military as an electrical engineer. Took my time. Knew it was always a possibility that I'd go back to medical school. My dad was a doctor. His father was a doctor, and so on. I'd majored in biology, so I was kind of pre-med even back then. I decided on surgery, which was much more of a challenge in terms of time. Residency was 120 hours a week, easily, but the department was supportive and fantastic." He paused. "I typically just tell people I preferred fixing them from the inside, instead of going into the entire spiel, but I've had some whiskey, weigh three-quarters what I used to, and haven't eaten today. I know you've all heard this before. Except for Lysha."

"What branch?" asked Reef. "I don't think I've ever asked you that."

"Army. I don't think I've ever asked you yours."

"Same."

"Where?"

"Fort Dix. And then Palestine when we went in."

"Shit."

"Yeah." Reef nodded, looking down.

"How'd you do it?" Lysha asked, glancing at

Reef.

He wrinkled his brow. "Do what?"

"You're a Muslim. Wasn't that impossible for you?"

Reef paused, and for a moment Lysha's expression was one of regret. She seemed to wonder if she'd gone too far in asking. "I became a Muslim after I left Palestine," he said.

Sy just listened from his perch against the wall. It'd taken him time to process the things Reef had told him about his time in the service. It seemed hard enough with just the two of them, filling the troughs with wood chips outside on a September night, passing the time with conversation.

"What about your experience made you change your religious views?" asked the doctor.

"Just being there. Seeing the carnage."

Joseph blinked.

"I converted to Islam after I got home. When my time comes, I'll pay for the things I did. But I try not to think about that, you know? I just try to live the best life I can, in Allah's eyes. And when He judges me, I hope He can see that I have tried to carry my sins with me, that I've tried to atone for them. But in our religion, I must find the people I've wronged, or their family, so that they may pass judgment on me. But because that is practically impossible, I can only pray for forgiveness and hope for mercy. I'll be punished, even in the afterlife. I've made my peace with that."

"I'm sorry you've had so much on your conscience for so long," said Lysha. "If it's any consolation, I believe that if there is a God—and I'm sorry if that's blasphemous to say to you—He'll have mercy on the fact that you're a good soul."

"I pray for that every day and night."

"Do these make you feel ashamed?" Lysha rubbed the spot between her shoulder blades where the microchip had been implanted during her time at the warehouse.

"No. For that, they burn." If words could kill, Reef would've ended every internment at once.

"For all of the unthinkable shit we've had to see," Joseph held up his drink. He closed his eyes and finished the whiskey. "It's fitting that you gave me this gift tonight. Just a game of cards, chance, and skill. Sometimes you're in the opportunistic position of getting a good hand. Sometimes you're better than the other person, and for whatever reason, they just get better cards. And there's nothing we can do about it."

"They're using a stacked deck," Lysha said. "What the hell do we do about that?"

"What we've been doing," Sy said, breaking his silence. "It's all we can do. You just have to hope you survive it." He ran a hand across his midsection. He could feel his ribs more than ever. "I remember learning that half of my grandfather's family had been wiped out in Dachau. I used to think, how the hell did those guys feel? You know? Shit, the Japanese, right here. Ireland before all that. Argentina later. So many. So many times. You see all the pictures, and yet there are still people smiling. You can see their hearts beating through their goddamn chests and yet they are *still smiling*. Still being human. And to think . . . *it couldn't have happened again.*"

"I'm older than all of you," the doctor said. "My grandfather would tell me when I was a child all of the horrors of the war. He was from London. Liverpool, actually. Right off the boat. And I just thought, man, that could never happen anymore. Especially not here, not in America. And here we are. And sometimes, we still smile. Hell, even laugh."

"There may not be a God in the way some of us believe, but there is a reckoning for anyone who believes they're superior to someone else and then acts on it. And it'll come. We may be dead and gone. Long gone. And it may come in the form of literature and shame, but it'll come."

It was dark and quiet.

"Hopefully," the doctor added.

***

The comfortable bedtime temperatures keeping the vinyl beds cool and the rooms warm enough for just a blanket or two were coming to an end. Sleeping right on the beds, even without a blanket, or perhaps the blanket just on your legs, was tolerable. Still, Sy tried to appreciate what was left.

Summer nights could be worse than winter nights in some ways, and the tenants frequently found themselves sleeping outside on a blanket on the grass, draped in anything to fight off bugs but being feasted upon by mosquitos nonetheless. But for now, for just a little bit longer, the nights were still just cool enough.

But it didn't matter that night. Not for Sy, after the excitement of giving Joseph his gift. Instead, his mind did backflips. He thought about his parents and how they might be holding up. Where they might be. Who they might be with. Were they worrying about him constantly? Of course they were, and they were no spring chickens. Stress will kill ya. He hoped they'd found ways to cope. Hobbies. More friends.

With no real way of getting in touch or even knowing where someone might be imprisoned, it was all a big guessing game for them. And everything in the strangled media would point to Sy being just fine. He imagined all the other parents. Spouses. Children. The ones whose families didn't make it through. They must've believed all was, at least, semi-okay. Or maybe their denial helped them believe that. Were they ever informed of deaths? Or were they left to live in the dark until this may or may not end?

He thought about his dad, sometimes commuting two hours each way, every day, to put food in his kids' mouths. To rent a condo on Long Beach Island for a week every year so they could vacation. To buy enough of a house where they all had their own bedrooms, in a safe town, unlike his own upbringing, in an area of Brooklyn that gentrification hadn't quite touched yet. Sacrifice is a rite of passage when you decide to have a family, but some were better built for it than others. Yet Sy didn't understand how his father could fall for the government's bullshit. He betrayed his own oppression. Sy often wondered if the apple had fallen too far from the tree.

Mom was the disciplinarian. He couldn't shit without her knowing where he was. Her neurosis for her children drove his brother away, but it had the opposite effect on Sy. He didn't like it, per se, but he was a similar person to her in that way. Sy's hyper-vigilant, everybody-accounted-for instinct was just pure DNA and repetition, and the full realization of that came to fruition almost two thousand miles away. He was tethered to his mother, even this far from her. And he missed her dearly.

She hadn't told anyone how she'd voted at first—or *if* she had voted, something Sy had argued about with her relentlessly. "Well, if I don't like anyone, Seymour," she had said, "why should I vote for them? Why should I just throw my weight behind a face that does nothing for me?"

"Did you like anyone this time, Ma?" he had asked.

"Maybe."

And that had been it. Until the shit hit the fan. Until they were collecting people. *Collecting* people.

Against their will and murdering them if they fought it. Until it got real. Until news wasn't allowed at the White House anymore. Until it wasn't allowed on television anymore. Only cherry-picked broadcasts by the administration itself.

"Mom, I *need* to know. Did you vote?" he had asked.

"No," she responded, now obviously aware of the severity.

Better than if she had voted and made the wrong choice. It helped him so much to know that, somewhere out there, Mom was okay. She was with Dad. Stressed, killing themselves slowly with worry, but together and alive. Unless the day came where they started apprehending people who didn't vote at all. So far, by all reports, by Priscilla's own word, by Lysha's own word, that hadn't been the case, as long as they got in line. He hoped it would stay that way.

This notion helped him drift slowly to sleep. Except he didn't dream of Mom or Dad. He dreamt of Palestinian and Israeli children sprayed with bullets. He felt the spatter of blood and brain. He tasted it. His shirt was off, and the spray decorated his body and face like a Jackson Pollock painting. His hair was still just as long as it was now, but his ribs protruded sickeningly, and his muscle definition was all but gone. He was bones, with skin wrapped around them.

He was in Auschwitz then, digging a trench and burying everyone, throwing bodies on top of the shit and piss and woodchips. He wasn't in Auschwitz. He was in Limbo. And the LOTs were executing everyone. More spray. More brains. More bodies into the trenches.

"Take your doctor," Stretch said. Two faceless LOTs threw Joseph's body at Sy, knocking both of them backward into the trench beneath. Sy landed on bodies on top of bodies, and Joseph's corpse crashed on top of him. They smelled, not of death, but of Indian paintbrushes. Above, Mateo and Ramón threw dirt onto them. Then more bodies. He was being buried. "I'm still fucking alive!" he tried to scream, but no words came. He sank lower into the pile of bodies, brain, woodchips, shit, and piss. *I'm still alive!* he thought, but he couldn't yell. And then the blankets followed. Tenants used shovels to scoop piles of frayed orange blankets on top of him. Each pile buried him deeper and deeper, until he could only see through a tiny gap in everything above his body. That's when he saw Reef, in his fatigues, aiming a gun directly down into the tiny gap. Directly into Sy's face. He pulled the trigger.

Sy jumped so hard he slid off his bed and onto the concrete floor, slamming his elbow. The thunk was hollow, reverberating down to his pinky and ring fingers, which went numb.

"Fuck," he said. He hoped no one had heard his gymnastics, but Lysha rushed into the room and the embarrassment commenced. She turned on the lamp and saw Sy on a hand and knees, flexing his left hand. He was only in his underwear, hair tied back with a rubber band.

"You okay?" she demanded, clearly shaken. She pulled him up by his other arm, and he plopped onto the bed.

"I'm all right," he said, embarrassed, trembling slightly, still bending his arm and squeezing his fist. "A dream."

"You mean nightmare?"

"Fucked me up." He indicated his body. "My legs are shaky."

"It's okay." Her arm wrapped around his shoulders. "You're okay."

He nodded. "It's like waking up from a nightmare into a fucking nightmare." He looked around and grunted. "Nightmares weren't so bad when you'd wake up at home." He thought on that. "The fuck is home anyway? I'd be gaining equity if I owned this place."

"I'm rentin', baby," she said.

They both laughed.

"I don't plan on buying property around here. Nuh-uh. Gonna lose its value real quick one day," she persevered.

"You can rent it to the LOTs, then," Sy said.

"Know what?" she mused. "It's messed up. I've never been anywhere more beautiful. Too bad I'll never step foot in this fuckin' state again once we get out."

"I'm packing up, taking my parents to the

Bahamas. Blue skies, the beach, no stress," Sy said.

"You'll miss the change of season. Isn't that what they always say?"

"My ass, I will."

She looked behind Sy on the bed. "And not a bad ass for a white guy."

"I squat a lot." He smirked and shook his head at his own joke. "Also, I think I'm like a sixteenth Brazilian."

"I'm half."

"Well then, that explains your ass too," said Sy.

"Excuse me?"

"Hey, no double standard here."

She raised an eyebrow. "I *just* noticed your ass. That means you've *been* looking at mine."

"I've been in a prison for three years. It's either you or Reef. And I'm 90 percent sure he's not into that. So, I'm just playing the odds."

Lysha pulled Sy's face to hers and kissed him. She kissed him long, and he could feel her unwillingness to pull away, so he leaned in and wrapped his arms around her. After a few more seconds, she pulled away. Then she bit her bottom lip. The kiss was potent. Maybe it was the three years of hugging a steel tray of a bed. Maybe it was the dry, wooden lips of his ex-girlfriend before they'd finally ended things. But Lysha felt electric, and it took his breath away.

"That's a favorable reaction to checking out

your ass," he said.

"Shut up. Kiss me again."

So he did.

TEN

LYSHA'S EYES opened when Sy shifted his weight. "Sorry," he whispered. "I didn't know if you meant to fall asleep. And I also couldn't feel my arm."

"Do you want me to go back to my room?"

"Totally up to you. Do I *want* you to? No."

"Then I'll stay," she said, closing her eyes again.

He traced her profile with his eyes and then with the back of his hand. Her skin was as soft and gorgeous as it'd looked. He felt what he thought was a tiny scar just beneath her earlobe. So she was real.

"I just don't want anyone to give you shit in the morning, playful or otherwise, if they see you here with me."

"I can handle myself." She yawned. He could barely make her out. If it wasn't for that solitary light in the middle of the courtyard attached to the top of the speaker pole, it would be complete darkness. But the golden glow on her brown skin turned her into a bronze goddess. Some ageless figure superimposed next to him. He caressed her again, then lay back and folded his arms on his chest, wincing at the pain in his elbow.

Lysha reached up and pulled one of his arms, the good one, back over her. She burrowed into him and sighed. She smelled summery and sweet. "I, uh, haven't really touched anyone in a while. It's nice," he said.

"You leave a girlfriend behind?"

"Nah. We hadn't been together in a while. What about you?"

"Yes."

This made him jealous. A different life, a different world. "What's his name?"

"Sophie."

Confusion roiled him. Lysha giggled.

"She wasn't really a girlfriend. Not yet. But I liked her. Met her at work. Probably not the best idea, anyway." She yawned deeply again.

"Has it always been girls?" Sy asked, not quite sure if that was the way to phrase it.

"Does it matter?"

"Well, yeah. I mean, no, not really, I guess. Just didn't know if I'm the . . . first . . . you know."

She turned and looked back at him. "Don't flatter yourself."

"Hey!" He said it too loud, and quickly dropped his voice. "I just know that this place isn't exactly swimming with females your age or . . .

orientation."

"No, Don Juan, I'm not lesbian. I'm not really anything. I've been with two women. A few men. I like who I like."

"That's great."

"Thanks for the approval."

"I didn't mean—"

"And you think that's *hot*, not great," she corrected, and put her head back down on the bed.

"Well now, who's the one judging?"

"I'm rolling my eyes, in case you can't see."

"Last time I had anything serious," Sy volunteered, "was enough for me for a while. We met through a friend and she cheated on me after a few years. We were together almost five years, all told. College through our 20s. On and off, but more on. And she cheated a lot. In college. After college. Then with my brother."

"Jesus." Lysha flashed a look back at him—he could make out her wide eyes, barely.

"Yeah, she liked military men. My brother was with his current wife, too. Family parties were always exciting."

"Did he know you knew?"

"No." He shook his head. "I wouldn't give him that satisfaction. He knew I'd found out she'd cheated, but that was all. Hell, everyone knew. And I never showed him I was hurt. I'd take it out on myself. I . . . have a temper sometimes. It was hard to control then. Just toxic." He was tired, fading with each word. "Anyway, after that, I just slept around for a little while, then enjoyed being alone." A deep breath. "Thought I'd figure myself out and then give it a shot again." He closed his eyes and opened them again. "By then, everything had started going to hell. And here we are."

"Here we are." She rested her head back down. "And did you figure yourself out?"

Sy closed his eyes again before he got to answer, and when he woke up, it was July.

He slept with only a thin blanket over the vinyl bed to prevent sticking. He stood up and stretched and drank a cup of water. He brushed his teeth with the new toothbrush Davey had brought him a few weeks before. The one before that had been two years old. He had brushed as gently as he could, but the bristles had gone to shit—he tried not to think about how unsanitary it was. But it was better than nothing. Maybe. Davey also brought them toothpaste, and for the first time in almost three years, Sy's mouth felt genuinely clean. Before that, he'd been using water and a small amount of salt from whatever packets he could gather. The abrasiveness helped clean his teeth—and probably rubbed off most the enamel, which explained the sensitivity. When he was desperate, he simply used soap. The taste lingered, but the suds would help, and the soap bar was somewhat readily available.

The toothpaste was spearmint, and Sy might

have eaten it had he no self-control. He wanted to brush down his throat into his esophagus. He brushed three or four times a day for the first week.

"Do you think you could fit a shower in that backpack next time?" he had asked Davey.

"I wish I were a magician."

"Pretty sure you are."

Sy spit into the sink and rinsed the residual toothpaste away with a handful of cold water. He splashed his face and used an old blanket to dry himself. Next, he gave himself a whore's bath and applied women's deodorant—it was one from the dozen Davey was able to procure. He couldn't have cared less.

He yawned big again and shook his head. He snatched a clean t-shirt from the back of the wooden chair and walked out into the common room, where Chandra and Sejal were singing songs.

"Sejal, how'd you sleep?"

"Hot," she responded instantly. She'd grown what seemed like a foot in only a few months.

He laughed. "Yeah, me too. How about you, Mom?"

Chandra just shook her head. She had gained weight over those same months. Sy had made sure of it, checking on her daily. Her depression had lifted as the weather warmed and she started spending more time with Sejal (and, in turn, Santi) in the process.

There were days he still found her sitting next to her son's grave, speaking to him in Hindi, laughing and crying. Sometimes Sy would bring her something to eat and walk the grounds with her. Other times, he would leave her to grieve. But he always kept an eye on the grave when he could, day and night, especially as the weather changed. The wildlife was hungry and ready to feast on anything. Nothing big enough was like to get over that fence without meeting Marlon Sr.'s fate, but he still made it a point.

Reef appeared from his room. "Sy, if you were Jamaican, you'd be a Rasta with all that hair. You ever gonna cut it? I mean, we have scissors now, ya know?"

Sy pulled the t-shirt over his body. "Listen, we cut our hair and they'll turn this place upside down looking for those scissors. And you should talk with all that wig."

"At least I can grow a man's beard."

"I'm evolved." Sy pushed through the front door just as the courtyard speakers sounded some garbled semblance of an alarm, the traditional warning of an incoming message. CJ was getting in an early-morning jog before the sun could burn him. He ran shirtless around Limbo and stopped in his tracks the moment the static choked through. The National Anthem blared. Sy and CJ met somewhere in the middle, both wondering aloud what the message would be this time.

"Hello, fellow Americans," it said. *"This is your monthly update."* Alarms blared again, awakening anyone who hadn't already been disturbed by the first

one. *"We are making great progress with our SLRs. We have rehabilitated hundreds of thousands of Americans who are back in society, functioning as though they'd never left. The success rate for someone who goes through an SLR is astronomically high. Tremendously high. If you're tired of . . ."* The speaker cut out for a moment. *". . . Then it's time you come home to your fellow Americans.*

"The upcoming SLRs will take place on August 8, as we are implementing a new monthly calendar for them instead of the usual quarterlies. This now gives you frequent opportunities to do the right thing.

"I'd also like to congratulate the Loyalist Party for boasting the highest percentage of registered voters in American political party history."

"That's because we're all in here, you fucking imbecile," CJ yelled at the speaker.

"The conflict in Palestine is more successful than ever, and we are truly bringing peace to a region that has been in conflict for over nearly one hundred years!

"We will slowly withdraw troops and let Israeli fighters take their place with a game-plan going forward. Israel is rightfully excited at the almost complete and flawless victory and looks forward to a peaceful future without the constant threat of terror and evil.

"As we ask every time, please join us in our new and, once again, great America. It only gets better and better. It would be lovely for all of you to remember what it feels like to sleep on a real mattress again, eating home-cooked food with your families who await your arrival. It's been long enough. Sign up with your local Loyalist Organization Troopers, and

get the process started.

"God Bless us all, and God Bless America."

The speaker crackled and went off air. Sy looked around at the tenants who'd crowded nearby. Most just hung out of their windows. "Fuck your mother," George in Building 7 yelled. He spat from the second floor.

"They're moving the SLRs from quarterly to monthly because they're tired of supporting our asses," said CJ. "They're going to aim for a burst of signups, maybe even go twice a month, all while slowly cutting back on supplies for all of us." He panned around the Limbo and shook his head. "Shit is about to get bad. Worse."

Sy stood silent, his brain on overload but his mouth full of glue.

"We're going to have to ration more," said CJ. "Stretch things out. When was the last truck? Monday? I'm going to keep a ledger of when they come. I'll bet dollars to doughnuts they start extending the delivery times. Cutting back on the heat in the winter. Electricity. Water, eventually. They're going to smoke us out or let us die."

"Let's not get ahead of ourselves," Sy finally said. "Maybe they're not getting the SLR signups they figured they would when they instituted them. Maybe they're getting desperate."

"Desperate for what!" CJ said. "They've got everything they've ever wanted, and none of us to stand in the way. Putin is dead. Merkel is long gone.

Macron is gone. The UN kissed the ring. Trudeau is the only opposition left, if he's even still around. They've won. They won ten years ago. They won eighteen years ago, when we elected Obama." CJ angrily threw a rock at the speakers and missed. "And even if they were desperate, who gives a shit? They'll still try to smoke us out. If they kill more of us, what do they care? If we're not aligning with them, we're useless anyway. It's fucking over, man."

Sy slinked away as CJ deliberated with himself. He pulled Reef to the side. "Did you hear that?"

"Most of it, why?"

"CJ is losing his shit, but he's got a point."

"Which is what?"

Sy beckoned Reef close to the fence, away from everyone else. "He thinks they're going to smoke us out, so to speak. Force us to take the SLRs by cutting us off."

"Why wouldn't they have just done that earlier?"

Sy mulled this over. "Because the cat-and-mouse game is done now. They're in control. They got us. They succeeded in whatever it was they wanted to do. We're all here. Maybe they're tired of allocating the money for this. So either we become their model citizens, scarlet-lettered cretins, or we die. Win-win." He pointed at the crack in Building 5's foundation—a zigzag that certainly meant structural failure. "You think they're going to fix something like that? No. That's eventually going to get worse, and the entire wall is going to fall in. Maybe the building collapses. We're on borrowed time no matter how you look at it. A year. Maybe two. Then what?"

"We'll waste away to nothing."

"We're already wasting away. Look at this." Sy dragged his fingernails along his forearm. Some of the skin flaked away. "I can't shit properly anymore. I get confused trying to remember things that should be second-nature." He ran his fingers through his hair and pulled out a small handful. "And the most fucked up part? I'm not even hungry half the time."

Reef stared him in the eyes.

"We're dying, man," Sy said. "Every day, faster and faster. We're just dying. And there's only so much Davey can do for us. For how many people out there, East Coast to West. We've *got* to fucking do something." He looked around and led Reef forward. "Come here." They walked toward the bushes until they reached the fence. He pulled back the section he'd breached by slowly breaking free the rungs and then replacing them precisely. It had taken him months to make that flap.

"How?" was all Reef could say.

Sy kicked some dirt underneath the bush, exposing a small hacksaw. "There are more blades under it. It takes me about two or three to get through one of the rungs. Another few months, if that, and we can squeeze out of here."

"And go where?" Reef asked, his eyes locked

on the fence. His expression seemed both shocked that Sy would do this and impressed at the same time.

"The border is five hundred miles away, give or take. We could get there in weeks on foot."

"You've finally lost it."

Sy didn't flinch.

Reef continued. "We'll never make it, for one. The LOTs drive that route all day, every day. You think they're that dumb? You think people haven't attempted the same thing?"

"I've already spoken in detail about it with Davey. He knows ways around it."

Reef chuckled. "You're going to trust a kid who only just learned his own way around? It's only a matter of time before that dude gets his noggin exploded all over the plains."

"Davey works for them. He knows their ins and outs."

"He knows what he thinks he knows. But he's a brash and cocky son of a bitch. I love him, but he's asking for it." He sighed. "You and everyone else underestimate these people, Sy. They're dangerous and they're in control. If they were as stupid as everyone calls them, would we be in here? For this long?"

Sy didn't have an answer. "Look, Davey and this"—he kicked the fence—"are all we've got. What else? We sit here and die?"

Reef paced the dry grass. "Let's say this works." He kept his voice low. "You and I get out.

We get to the border. Great. What happens to everyone else? To Joe? To CJ? To *Lysha*?"

"We come back," he answered without hesitation. "We get ourselves healthy and in order, get established for a few weeks, and we come back."

"You're telling me you can't shit and your body is falling apart and you want to make multiple five-hundred-mile round trips on foot, back to a place where the LOTs will almost certainly be waiting for us. What if they decide to start shooting motherfuckers up because of us?"

Sy didn't have an answer. "I'm not talking about leaving tomorrow. I'm talking about having a conversation. And if you can think of something better, I'm all ears." He bent over and double-checked the fence, rearranging the branches. "Look, I love you man, and I trust you more than probably anyone I've ever known. I shared this with you because of that. I don't think there's anyone on this planet I respect more than you. I figured you'd know that by now. I'm simply trying to figure it out. I want you to help me. I think the two of us could change this." He peered around the compound. "Maybe not all of it. Maybe just some of it. Maybe even none of it. But I can tell you I'm ready to die giving it a shot. Because I'm not ready to die here. I'm not going to die here. I'm dying on the other side of that fence, one way or another, in my freedom. On my land. I don't care if they take me out the second I start walking away. It *won't* be in this motherfucking dump."

"Is your land Canada?"

"If Canada needs to be my land until I can get back to my life, so be it. Would you rather waste away? Die of a staph infection, rotting away on that fucking thin-as-a-ball-sack mattress? Or on a whim by some backwoods fuck who has no idea what it's like to actually serve this country, never mind see the things you've seen? Some *Deliverance* motherfucker who shoots you in the back because you're black and he felt like being a hero to his other toothless cohorts, spitting juice into a peach-tea Snapple bottle from their packed lips. Or—"

"No, Seymour, that's not what I want," Reef cut him off. "Do you think that's what I want? More dead babies. More people losing their shit? You think I want to spend year-in and year-out going through Ramadan while numb to my toes or throwing up because of the heat, with no food in my stomach?" He backed away from the fence. "But I won't put these people at risk for my own selfishness."

Sy looked around them, concerned the others would overhear. "I'm not being selfish."

"And I'm not saying you are. But I feel that I would be. I can't abandon my people. We're the front lines here, and I have to hold it down for them."

"You're the one who told me to get out of here! It was your idea!" He paused, trying to relax. "All I'm asking you to do is think about it. Maybe even come up with something better. Just give me that much." Lysha appeared in the doorway of their building. "Please."

"I wanted you to leave legitimately, because I think you have the best chance of getting through the SLRs." He rubbed his eyes. "Yes, yeah, I'll think about it. Only because it's you, Sy."

"You guys all right?" Lysha asked, approaching. Her tank top was navy blue and snug to her body. She wore cargo pants and a pair of black boots laced all the way up that disappeared under the cuffs of the pants. Her hair was, as usual, in two buns. "Some of us could hear you guys from all the way in there."

Sy's face warmed. "*What* could you hear?"

"Nothing specific. Just sounded intense. Wanted to make sure you guys weren't going to throw some hands out here."

"Sy doesn't want none of this," Reef said.

"You're right. I'm too brittle now."

"Oh, I was looking forward to watching two alphas duking it out." She fanned her face with her hand. "What else could a girl ask for?"

"Really?" asked Reef, the sun shining in his eyes, making him wince.

"No, man. I can't stand when two doofuses try to piss on their territory."

"What if they piss on each other?" Sy asked.

"That's some freaky shit." She pondered it. "I might be into it."

Sy stuck out his bottom lip and blinked

rapidly. "I'm going back inside."

"Freaky boy," Lysha called after him.

"Yeah, freaky boy!" Reef yelled as Sy opened the door, shaking his head and laughing to himself.

ELEVEN

THE TWO thuds were muffled, but everyone in the common room jumped. Reef and Sy charged out the front door. They turned the corner of the building, following where the noise had originated, and stopped in their tracks. On the ground, necks broken and blood and brain leaking from their skulls, were Santiago's mother and father. They'd jumped from the roof, diving headfirst onto the concrete. The woman moved, twitched, and lifted her head about two inches off of the ground before she tried to lift her torso. She collapsed and didn't move again.

Footsteps descended on them from the front of the building, and Reef turned to stop anyone from seeing. "No. Stay here," Sy heard him say. He turned to help, letting Reef rush to the bodies. His triage skills were light-years ahead of Sy's, and though Sy knew the couple was as dead as anyone could be, he still wanted to get Joseph.

Mateo tried to push past Sy, but Sy held

strong. "I promise, you don't want to see it. Make *sure* Santiago does not see anything. Go find him and keep him inside."

"Wait, who . . ."

"Lisa and Ramón. They jumped off the roof."

"How the fuck did they even get up there?" Mateo asked.

"A window upstairs, I guess. I don't know. Just stay here, please, and take care of Santi. There'll be a crowd soon. Can I trust you?"

Mateo froze.

"Yo." He gave Mateo a shake on the shoulders.

"Yes," Mateo said.

Sy sprinted past Building 8 and across the yard. His feet were suddenly heavy. He felt a sharp pain in his chest and collapsed face-first onto the grass in front of Building 6.

***

When Sy awoke, the leaves were scattering from the trees and blowing all around the courtyard. Orange and red and yellow and brown. The autumnal breeze brought with it the smell of death—the annual death of the deciduous trees, the death of grass and bushes, the death of warm and sustaining temperatures. One of the small benefits of early October in Wyoming was the comfortable sleeping temperatures, but it was the beginning of the end, and each tenant knew that. The comfort would quickly shift to bitter cold.

Sy stood with his arms crossed as the leaves swirled around him. His hair—now with a few strands of white—and patchy beard blew in the windy courtyard. His gaze was locked on a particular tree that seemed to be shedding all of its leaves right then and there, unwilling to wait for the rest of its peers. He was in his usual white thermal shirt, gray sweatpants, and black boots. He blinked the irritation away from his eyes as his immune system fought the pollen in the only way it knew how: a dripping nose, a dry throat, and stinging eyes.

The doctor put his arm around Sy, and then patted his belly. "Good to see you this way."

Sy coughed out a chuckle.

"Has the guilt receded?" the doctor asked.

"Not really."

"They have enough to eat. That's why you all rationed. You need it. Would you rather be dead?"

"Is that a rhetorical question?" Sy's arms fell to his side.

CJ had been right those few months back; the days and weeks between food shipments were beginning to expand. Not extreme at first, but for those who rationed out the meals, they certainly noticed.

"How has your breathing been?"

"A lot better."

"And your chest?"

"Same."

Whether or not Sy had had a heart attack, Joseph couldn't be sure, though he doubted it. What he did know was that the man was overly stressed, which in turn likely caused the chest pains that took him off his feet. After a few days' rest, Sy was back up and at it, but he didn't feel the same. That was when Lysha and Joseph noticed the portions he'd rationed off for himself were less-than-sustainable for his body and health. It took some stealthy work, but with the help of CJ, they had tracked him over the course of a week. Sy denied it when confronted, but ultimately couldn't lie to people who had gone that far out of their way to help him. He admitted he'd cut down on calories to make more for the others in his building. Lysha started to bring him his portions every day, watching him and making sure he'd eat it all.

"I feel like a toddler."

"You look like one, these days," she responded.

Then came Davey. He'd managed a gigantic tub of weight-gainer. It didn't taste fantastic mixed with water, but it certainly worked. Sy had bounced back within a month or so. Not to be undone, though, he shared the shakes with Chandra and a few others who were in desperate need of more calories. Santi had moved in with her and was a growing boy, requiring more and more food every day. And Sejal didn't do so bad herself. Every month, Davey brought another tub of the powder, and every month

Sy would empty it into some sort of food packaging and place it in inconspicuous places with the other food, so as not to be raided by the LOTs when they did their random visits (these had also become much rarer). Hidden in plain sight.

The last raid had been at the beginning of August, where they'd found a bottle of Advil in Joseph's room. He'd forgotten to hide it after using it for his own migraine the night before.

"Where did you get this?" Em the LOT asked him.

"It's one of the ones you guys give us."

"No it's not. We give individual packets, and you know that. Now, I'm going to ask you again where you got this." She had shaken the bottle in Joseph's face as she stepped up closer to him. Little did she know that Joseph was a master of the straight face.

"I told you, I got it from you guys. This was more than a year ago. I don't know why we got a full bottle, but it came with some antibiotics we asked for. Seymour put in the request and this is what I received. I don't know what else to tell you."

Fatty Arbuckle had accompanied her into the room, and when she looked at him, he just nodded to the door.

"I'll tell you what. I'll say I believe you." She opened the bottle and tossed the capsules across the room by shaking them out. "I don't, but I'll tell you I do. If I hear your name again, or find something else of this nature, I'll make sure you're made an example of. And if we catch who brought you these meds, we'll make sure they pay dearly, as well. So I'd warn them if I were you."

Joseph nodded smugly.

When she left, the doctor picked up the capsules, one at a time. The pills were a hot commodity, depending on what Davey could get and when he could get them. A little bit of floor grime wouldn't hurt their integrity.

It was the end of November when Sy finally freed enough rungs to be almost certain that he (and anyone else) could fit through the fence. As he moved farther from the original rung he'd managed to break through the year before, the less and less corroded the others were. Some would take days to cut through. Without a true schedule of LOT appearances—and best believe CJ tried his damnedest (and failed) to figure out a pattern to their driving routes—it was next to impossible to confidently work for any serious length of time. So, just like Andy Dufresne, Sy slowly carved his way through that fence, kick by kick. Hacksaw blade by hacksaw blade.

When it was big enough to fit a person through, he found himself crying.

He cried in relief that he hadn't been caught.

He cried because he finally had an out if he wanted to take it.

He cried because he was petrified the LOTs

would discover it and not only secure it, but punish everyone for his indiscretions.

He'd own it. There was no hesitation in his mind, not for a moment. But he wondered if that would matter.

He cried because his life over the last nearly four years felt like a dream. When he came in at twenty-six, he *knew* he would be out as soon as the country got its shit together. Four years? Impossible to imagine. Yet, there he was, staring down the barrel of a life sentence, never mind a few years.

He cried because there was nothing he could do about it.

He cried because maybe there was.

He cried with his head against that fence, his tears dripping down onto the cold steel.

When Lysha touched his shoulder, he jumped and wiped his face furiously. His cheeks were red, his eyes puffy. He looked away.

"You know," she began, "when I came here, I thought I was going to have to fight for myself. I thought I would have to battle for my body. And my mind. That it was going to be some free-for-all of desperate, emaciated people, and that any fresh meat would be stalked and devoured in time. Instead, I found a community of people surviving. Some thriving." She shrugged. "Others getting by. But *surviving*. A small commune of good people who wouldn't harm a soul. Who cared for each other. Locked up like animals while the beasts roam free.

But it didn't matter, because they protected each other like family."

He turned back to her, eyes bloodshot and tears finding ways to escape no matter how he tried to hold them in. He reached out and took her face in his hand. She leaned into it. "People still died," he said. "Some because of things we could've done better to protect them."

"And people die out there every day. You can't save the world, Seymour. You can't save our world. This world." She held out a pointed finger at the buildings behind her. "No matter how few we may be, it's just not possible." She reached out and wiped his face. "Why do you torture yourself? What does this to you?"

"Something."

"*What* is that something?" she asked, assuming he had to know.

"I wish I had an answer. These fucks did this to us to bring us to our knees, in more ways than one. It gave me purpose. I used to think I've become a different person than I was before, but this just whittled away the bullshit part of me. Everyone here drives me. Not letting this place beat us is what pushes me. I care too much about you all."

She sighed and wrapped the blanket she'd cloaked herself in tightly around her body. "Everyone cares about people. Even the hardest of the hard loves someone. A man who kills and eats his victims loves his mother. Or father. Or kid. It's just too general to say that. You have something in here"—she patted his chest—"that not many others have. This . . . drive. What is driving you?"

"You."

She wrinkled her brow.

"Reef. Joseph. Mateo. Chandra. Siva. Ramón. *Marlon*." He caved with the last name on the list. It brought him to his knees on the soil, where underneath him were the graves of some of his list. Lysha reached out and touched his shoulder, and he trembled as he sobbed. He touched the earth, where it was more loose than the surrounding dirt.

Marlon's final remains had tumbled off the razor wire during a wicked summer storm. His bones scattered outside of the fence, and when the LOTs discovered him, they laughed as they tossed the remnants of a desperate father out into the brush in front of them like they were tossing branches that had fallen from a dead tree. Sy begged them to stop, begged to Stretch and his cronies. He asked them to give him the remains, so his people could give the man a proper burial. But they just kept on throwing and laughing at Sy's demand.

And then Sy snapped. It was the sheer level of disrespect that another human being could display on purpose. He lurched at the fence, grabbed with both hands and shook it. "Listen to me you cocksucking hick bastard. If you don't give them to me I swear to God I will cut your fucking hearts out if I ever have the chance. You fucking slobs."

CJ bear-hugged Sy and dragged him off the fence, but Sy fought through his grasp until Reef got there and was able to wrangle him back. "Seymour, shut up. Stop. Just stop. What the hell is this going to do for anyone?"

Sy didn't hear a word. The shade of red he saw was crimson and had permeated his brain and body, a virus of rage, and he continued fighting through their grasps like the animal the LOTs told him he was. Then Stretch looked him dead in the eyes and smiled a shit-eating grin that bared all the teeth in his mouth. He lifted a bone, tossed it on the ground, and took his cock out. He pissed on it. Sy screamed a primal yell. He reversed his course and ran to the back of the building, where he picked up a piece of the broken chair that had lived in the same spot since he showed up to Limbo 5-8. He sprinted back to the fence, holding the piece of wood over his head like a javelin, the splintered end of it pointing outward. He stabbed it through the fence, at Stretch, who was zipping his khaki uniform pants.

"Must've been all that beer I had last night," Stretch said aloud right before the spear stopped short of his head by about three inches. The wood wedged itself in between the rungs at its base. Again CJ snatched Sy from behind. This time, Reef got between the two of them. When he turned to reason with Stretch, the trooper's revolver went off, blowing a hole in Reef's side. He dropped to the ground and Sy broke free again. This time, Lysha stepped in his way. She didn't bother to turn to the LOT. She simply stared Sy in his red face, the sweat beading off his forehead. The rage in his eyes quieted as he swallowed it back down into his gut. That's when he noticed Reef. He tore the shirt off of his body and dropped to his knees.

The LOTs got in their truck and peeled away. Sy was sure he'd heard one of them yell at the other, "The fuck, man?"

"Reef, Reef—you okay?" He searched to find where on Reef's body the bullet had hit. He pulled up Reef's shirt, where the blood had pooled some. Then he saw the flesh wound along his ribs. It had taken some meat with it, but the bullet hadn't come anywhere near anything important.

"I'm okay, I think," Reef said, attempting to sit up.

"Stay down, Joseph is here," CJ said to Reef as the doctor made his way through, the gunshot having alerted him.

"Joe, he's okay. It's just a flesh wound. It's just a flesh wound. He's okay. Right? He's okay, right?"

"Let him get in there, Sy," Lysha said, guiding him back.

Sy wiped his face with the back of his hand, smearing blood across his cheek and forehead. He put his hands on his hips. "He's okay, Joe. I'm telling you. He's okay."

The doctor looked up at Sy, who was still

trembling. "Go inside and sit. Get some water, and I'll be there as soon as I bring him back to my place and stitch him up. He's okay, Sy." He looked over at Lysha, and she took the cue.

She wrapped her arm around Sy's. He trembled, the adrenaline leaving his body, coursing its way out through every strand and fiber of muscle and nerve. She led him to Building 8 as he looked back at Reef. "I'm sorry, Reef," Sy said. "I'm sorry."

The doctor sat Reef up and was getting ready to lift him to his feet. It was only when Sy climbed the few steps to the front door that he noticed the bullet track running along the front of the building, gouging the concrete along its path, and disappearing on the other side.

That night, after the doctor tended to Reef (and opted not to stitch him after all), he visited with Sy, who'd calmed and ended up sleeping for a few hours before waking up mostly composed. The two of them took a walk outside to get some air on a cool summer night. "Is Reef angry with me?" he asked.

"Not in the least. He's concerned about you. He mentioned something about the gate, Sy, and I have to say, I'm getting a bit alarmed with your thought processes lately . . ." He stopped. Sy had locked in on something near the fence where he had watched his friend get shot a few hours earlier. As he got closer, he recognized the bones. They were strewn about where someone had tossed them back over haphazardly. But they were there, most of them, including Marlon's skull. Sy turned and looked back at Joseph, who was just as awestruck.

"Who . . .?"

Sy shook his head.

"Davey?"

"He wouldn't just sneak around like this. He's calculated. If the LOTs take another ride around and see these here . . ." His perplexity gave way to concern. "Joe, help me get these somewhere safe."

The two men moved the bones into the bushes near Building 5, where Sy could bury them early in the morning before the sun came up, next to Siva and Priscilla and the others.

When he returned inside and walked through the common room, Reef called out from his bedroom, a mere whisper. Sy tiptoed in.

"I didn't know you had it in you," Reef said.

"Reef, I'm so sorry, man, I just . . ."

"Lost your shit." He laughed and tried to stifle it, then sat up at the edge of his bed. "It's just everything boiling up inside of you. But you've got to vent it. Otherwise, the top blows off and today happens. You gotta let it out slowly. The damn pushups and sit-ups aren't enough." He shifted his weight and winced. "I want you to meditate with me, man."

"You know I don't really do the religious thing."

"I'm not talking about praying, Sy, I'm talking about meditating. Releasing some of that stress.

You're going to kill someone. Or yourself. Listen, if I mention turning you into a Muslim even once, you can take off. All right?"

"I owe you that much, I suppose."

"You almost owed me a kidney. Or spleen. Or whatever the fuck is over here." He pointed to just beneath his rib on his left side. "Served in a fucking war and didn't get shot. Took a damn white dude losing his damn shit in a prison camp to do it. Tell the me of five years ago that story and I'd . . ." He thought. "I'd probably believe it. That's sad, isn't it?" He tied his hair back using a few of his dreads. "Come and sit. I'm going to teach you how to breathe."

When Sy stood from his knees, he wiped his pants clean and shook his head, trying to clear his brain. Lysha wiped his face clear of tears.

He stood in front of everything he'd tried to protect and provide for. He stood in front of what had become home. He stood in front of Lysha, who studied him. He knew what this life was. But he had forgotten what the life out there, behind him, was. Even though it wasn't the same life he knew before, it was still *out there.*

"A few weeks walk," he remembered telling Reef. The two had never discussed it again. The time would come, and when it did, he'd worry about it. It was rapidly turning into another winter. Another brutal winter. He'd never survive the journey in that

weather, especially not as he moved north, navigating a land he was unfamiliar with. And then a border that was likely flooded with LOTs making sure no one had a chance of getting through. He'd have to meticulously plan every single move, every resting point, absolutely everything.

Lysha raised his chin, forcing him to look her in the eyes, and then she took both of his hands. "I think you're the strongest person I've ever met. And I want to go with you," she said.

How did she know? he thought. "Go where?"

"Anywhere."

Maybe he wouldn't have to do it alone.

TWELVE

CHRISTMAS DAY was the same as any other winter day in Limbo: cold and uncomfortable. It didn't exist to the group in the same ways that other religious holidays didn't exist, en masse. Reef observed Ramadan himself—in years past by calculating the days in his head, and now with the aid of Davey (which, consequently, taught him that he'd had the last two years off by a week or two each time). Chandra and Sejal celebrated Diwali themselves. Lysha celebrated a semi-secular version of Christmas along with CJ and Joseph. Other denominational tenants in other buildings held masses of their own. Tiny churches in tiny rooms.

Sy didn't celebrate anything, but he appreciated all of it. He spent time asking questions about everyone's habits and rituals. He learned about things he never would have asked before being placed in Limbo. Like the process behind arranged marriages and what Hindu weddings are like. Or specifically *when* people opened their Christmas gifts, on Christmas Eve or Christmas morning?

More than anything, what the tenants celebrated in a big way were birthdays. They saw them as the biggest milestone—another year surviving Limbo. Each person was celebrated by a chorus of tenants singing Happy Birthday from each building on the compound. Limbos 1-4 and 9-12 might even join in, and vice versa. Each birthday was a symbol of beating the evil for another year. And for a day, maybe even just a few hours of that day, some people forget all about being inside. They were surrounded by people who loved them and cherished their time together.

Birthdays were the real holiday—and it just so happened that Sy's birthday fell on Christmas Day. The Jew with the Christmas birthday sounded like a children's book, but it was a common refrain amongst his friends and other tenants. Sy joked that he'd benefited from it all his life, because he'd get gifts on Christmas Day after all.

Christmas that year was like the one before it and the one before that—until sunset. Reef and Lysha, who had acquired candles from Davey for everyone's birthday (they only used one candle for each birthday and could use each candle a bunch of times) devised the typical Limbo birthday cake for Sy: a piece of cornbread. Once in a while, they'd get their hands on a piece of pound cake in the food delivery, and, if possible, they might have Davey fetch a cupcake.

But this year, it was the norm. Lysha pushed the candle into the stale cornbread and pulled a match to light it. Before she had the opportunity to strike the match, the speakers in the courtyard rang out their typical alarm to prepare for an announcement. But it was dark. This was anything but typical.

A bit of feedback shrieked through before the national anthem blared. It was a varied version of the song, the tone skewed and the pitch distorted. The tenants all made their way through the front door and out into the fresh inch of snow that had fallen throughout the day and was still accumulating. Most rubbed their arms to warm up. Sy wrapped his coat around Chandra and Sejal.

As the anthem neared its end, it was abruptly interrupted by a peculiar laughing. The laughter was intentional, not someone leaning on a wrong button.

"That fucking song." The voice was clearly run through a changer. *"How many of you sons of bitches are tired of hearing it? How many times has it woken you up in the morning when you're exhausted because you can't sleep from the heat? Or from the cold? Or from the bugs? Or from the mice and rats? Or from the asshole in the room next door who won't stop crying? Or sniffling? Or coughing? It's not even been the national anthem for a century. That was a bastardized version of 'God Save The Queen.' Real creative.*

"If you're listening to this, then you're where we once were. Some of us a while back. Some more recently. Did they think they'd hold us all forever? It's 2026. And we're not

exactly dealing with Einsteins. Kudos to them for working it as long as they have, but it's collapsing on them. You don't know it, because you're sheltered in those sorry excuses for concentration camps, but we're here, friends. And we're growing by the day. We're taking the country back. Making it . . . well, you know.

"We know that some of you are petrified of finding a way out. They have you tracked. They watch you. The LOTs are always lurking around. You don't know where you are or where to go. No maps, no GPS, no phones, nothing. But we ask you this: Would you rather waste away in that hellhole and definitely die? Or would you rather give it a shot on the outside?

"Come find us. Not in Canada. Here, in America, where you belong. Where we belong.

"We are holed up in every major city in every state. Check the city halls. Check the libraries. We are out here. Everywhere.

"Fuck this administration and fuck their America.
"Merry Christmas."

A version of Silent Night played briefly before the sound cut with the same feedback it began with. Everyone stood around staring, as if the speakers were going to self-destruct.

"I don't buy it," CJ said from the back of the group. "They're trying to fuck with us. Playing games. Nope. They want to find out who the rats are. The traitors. Anyone who miraculously steps one foot outside of one of these Limbos in the next few days is good as dead."

"I don't know, CJ. What the hell *was* that

message?" Reef asked. "Are they even capable of something like that? It's not their style."

"Anyone is capable of putting on a performance like that . . . for the right amount of money." CJ paced. "There are probably LOTs outside of every single damn Limbo in the country and at city halls and libraries just waiting to put down the ballsiest and most idiotic prisoners. I wouldn't fall for it. And unless there are some flimsy-ass Limbos elsewhere in the country, I don't think they've noticed how hard it is to get out of one of ours."

"CJ is right," the doctor said. "Which way is out? Over the death wire? How'd that fare for Marlon? Or right through the gate, like a goddamn nutjob? How many times has CJ tried to disable that alarm? Or trigger the gate? How about we dig down deep enough, under the however-many feet of fence underground, using whatever debris we've saved over the years, and crawl out from underneath, just to have our heads stomped on by a bunch of sadistic jerk-offs on the other side?"

Sy finally opened his mouth. "Can we really suspect no one's gotten loose over all these years? I mean, think about the people we've been in company with. Look around here right now. You don't think there's a contingency of us who could make it on our own? I don't think it's too far-fetched to believe that factions of people are grouping together and disrupting this— this."

The snow fell faster and harder. Everyone had

a layer of it on their hair and hats. Most hugged themselves to keep from chattering.

"Or maybe there aren't enough people going through the SLR programs, and they're just weeding out those with ill intentions," CJ suggested.

"Then why not just walk in here and execute us?" Sy asked. "What's the point of making us break out of a nearly impossible situation, with hurdle after hurdle, after years of weakening us?"

"Because there are people who won't go through the SLRs who would jump ship if given the chance," Joseph said. "They're just too afraid of the SLRs themselves. How many people have come back from an SLR once gone?" No one said a word. "Exactly. So they're either getting out. Being *rehabilitated*." The sarcasm was thick. "Or they're just thinning the herd."

"Again," Sy said. "It makes no sense. Call the person's name, have them get in a truck, and execute them. Why does there have to be this elaborate plan when the end result is the same? They're not looking to waste any more money on us. It just doesn't feel like bullshit. It wouldn't make sense."

The crowd had mostly dispersed by then, the cold too much for them to bear. Sy found himself staring at the fence behind the now-naked bush. The sky was bright for a night sky, as it normally was while snowing. The compressors attached to each building kicked on as the heat blasted inside. Thus far, the heat had been as consistent as it had in years past.

"I don't think it means much for us, regardless," said CJ. "We're not exactly in some rinky-dink camp."

Sy flashed a look to Reef, who stared back knowingly. "But we're in agreement that we cannot continue the way we are forever. It's not sustainable." Everyone in attendance agreed in their own way. A head nod. A word. Body language. "So then what do we do? Who goes the SLR route and reports back after? Who tries to figure out a way to do it on their own?"

"We can take out the next batch of LOTs who deliver something to us," Mateo spoke up.

"Just kill them?" Sy asked. "Do you want to murder someone?"

"It's self-defense," said Mateo. "You telling me you'd feel bad for these people?"

Sy shook his head. Snowflakes fell from his hair. "I'm saying I'm not like them. And neither are you."

"Could've fooled me when you tried to spear that tall motherfucker a few months ago."

"'The irrationality of a thing is no argument against its existence, rather a condition of it'," Joseph said. "Nietzsche. I believe it's true. Always have. Sy releasing years of justifiable anger is no comparison to the sheer joy these men get out of tormenting us. And you certainly don't think killing troopers in front of cameras would be all that intelligent, do you?"

"I'll cut the fucking wires. Break the lens.

Where there's a will."

They were the only ones in the entire world, Sy recognized now. How desperately alone they were. They would need to fend for themselves, and he was deeply ready to do that. He was done, and he would rather die while trying to survive than barely survive while slowly dying. How much more dangerous could it be out there compared to sitting around, wasting away? Either could end in their demise, but one was for sure, unless something drastically changed. If any such shift was imminent, it wasn't obvious.

There was no way to know, but Sy was willing to bet on himself. He hoped others would be as eager.

Lysha appeared from behind the pack and leaned her head into Sy's shoulder, huddling into him for warmth. He wrapped his arm around her, and she looked up at him. "Anywhere."

He kissed the top of her head.

She nuzzled closer. "Happy Birthday."

THIRTEEN

IT WAS unseasonably warm for February. Fifty-five degrees, to be exact. The entire week had been abnormally warm, though no one was complaining. Sleeping was comfortable. Walking around and stretching out legs was bearable and even pleasant at high noon, the sun warming the tenants while they shuffled about, getting their blood flowing.

Sy stared at the fence in front of him. Not only had no one on the outside bothered it, but no one on the inside had noticed it, either. In recent weeks, he'd been able to tell that Reef was coming around to the idea of escaping. It didn't take words to figure that out. But Sy refrained from pestering him. After that initial conversation, he opted to give Reef the opportunity to approach him first.

Either the message on Christmas Day was real and undetectable, unnoticed by the LOTs and even the government itself, or the LOTs maintained poker faces and refused to acknowledge it. There had only been one announcement since that day, however, at the beginning of February, naming dates for the upcoming SLRs. There were no more details, nothing else said. The Star-Spangled Banner was still played, and George still spat from his window. But it was clear as day that they were running low on intros, as there had been vacant rooms for months. Strategy? Mind games? Not in Sy's eyes. Something was shifting, and he wasn't sure it was a good thing. Not for anyone locked inside, at least.

"It's crumbling," CJ said during a common room discussion. "They're pulling some bullshit to set us up."

"Smoking us out. You were right, my man. They're trying to smoke us out," said Reef. "All we have to do is pop that SLR pill and we're gone. No more cold. No more starving. No more fences. Sign that paper and you're gone, baby."

CJ exhaled slowly and shook his head.

"See how good that sounds? Simple," Reef said. "I'm curious how many other desperate souls just did it. Just up and did it and signed and now they're dead. 'Here's a warm meal for you, son.'" Reef mocked. "'Welcome back to civilization, glad y'all made the right decision and we're lucky to have you back. Go on and eat up and pick out a bed for a nice nap. Most people sleep like the dead after so many years on that rubber mat they call a mattress.' I can tell you I've been so damn desperate at times I've thought about it. But I'll sit here and starve to death before I give them the satisfaction. Before handing *myself* over without a fight. No. I'll go down swinging, thanks."

Sy had looked Reef right in the eyes and understood immediately.

And now Sy stood at that fence on a day where the sun felt incredible, and a bit of laughter could even be heard from open windows. He leaned against Building 5, hands behind his back, observing anyone who might walk by or be able to see him— out of frame of the security camera. When he was clearly alone, he took a few steps closer to the weakened area. He watched a LOT truck make its rounds, and then when the sun had begun to sink in the sky, bent down and pulled back the part he'd meticulously worked on for over a year using just the bottom of his boots, a tiny hacksaw, and a ton of elbow grease.

The fence bent back just enough for him to slide his feet through, and then the rest of his legs up to his waist. When he glanced up, he noticed Reef standing six feet away from him.

"Just gonna take off. No goodbyes. Nothing on your back."

"I'm not leaving," Sy said. "Just wanted to make sure I could fit. I didn't want to be banging around any more than I had to." He scooted farther back, clearing the fence up to his shoulders, then neck, and finally all the way out. He crawled from under the bush and pushed himself to his feet, dusting off his clothes.

Reef stared at him from inside. Sy stared back from outside. His heart raced in his chest. He was exhilarated. He looked down at the winter dirt and gently kicked a pile of it, watching the dusty earth disappear in the breeze. Why did it look different from this side? Because it was. It was free dirt. Just as free as he was in that moment. He looked back up at Reef.

"How does it feel?"

There were no words. Sy just placed his hands on the fence, followed by his forehead. He cried quietly, choking down sobs. He felt Reef's hands on top of his own, followed by his own forehead.

"If I never get this again, at the very least, I'll know I didn't forget how it feels." He backed off the fence and glanced behind him, at the brush and plains that stretched for what looked like eternity. He took a few steps away.

"Sy."

Sy didn't turn around. He only kept walking.

"Sy, come back through. Let's do this the right way."

He turned around. "I'll be back in a minute."

Reef's mouth was a straight line.

"I promise."

Sy stepped over sticks and through some shrubbery. Once he cleared it, he was out into the plains he had stared at for four years. The dormant grass was much longer than it looked from his window—it came up nearly to his knees. He listened for rattles even though it was winter, though the warm weather alarmed him a bit, and kept his eyes open as he trekked through the brush. John McLemore had long ago explained most rattlers in Wyoming lived in shorter grasses, and there were a lot fewer than people would assume. The idea of it scared him some, but dying out in the plains via Mother Nature scared him much less than in some concrete coffin of a room.

The sun changed the color of the sky as it hit portions of the horizon obscured by snow-covered mountains. An orange-pink glow emanated from underneath the clouds, which were low in the sky. Sandwiched between them and the peaks of the mountains was half of a fiery ball, casting rays out in every direction. The more distant the mountains, the more of a silhouette they were.

He pressed on. The only interest he had was ahead of him, and as the grass changed from tall and wild to tame and short, a dirt road manifested, perhaps forty or fifty yards out. He reached it in a hurried stride as the land dipped down. Then he stood in the middle of it. It was lighter in color than the surrounding land after being used year after year for patrolling. He should've been petrified, as exposed as he was, standing out in the middle of nowhere and visible for probably miles, especially on that straight shot of a road in both directions. But he wasn't. He was the most carefree he'd been since before his

Limbo tenure. Maybe ever.

What was startling was how quiet it was. Sure, it was a bit warmer than normal, but the wildlife wasn't any more active than it would have normally been this time of year. The noises of the camps were gone, and though he'd always been stunned at the hush of the area, this was something else. Dead, ear-ringing silence.

He pushed on and deeper out into the fields, dodging gnarled tree stumps and bushes along the way. Facing him was a hill in the shape of a cresting wave. It was more carved out of the surrounding land than it was conical, and only scalable from the backside. So that's where he found himself—walking around the seventy- or eighty-foot hill and climbing, slipping and sliding on the melting dirt, slick and now muddy. He struggled and clawed but finally reached the summit. Upon standing, he looked at his Limbo in the distance for the first time. The tears burned his eyes again, as he could see not only his own, but most of the surrounding Limbos. A line of ten camps, snaked slightly, offset. Limbo 5-8 was the last on the line, as he already knew, and the numbers likely meant it was the second built before they opted to go in the other direction for whatever reason, but when next to each other in that way, from that height, they all looked like one. At the end of the day, they were. Everyone in the same situation, going through some variety of the same problems. Only now Sy's problems were on the outside. And looking down on the only home and land he'd occupied for four years was equally sad and striking.

And very, very far out in the distance, Sy was sure he could see some lighting. More Limbos? Offices? Could've been a reflection of the sunlight on something metal, for all he knew.

As the sun dipped lower, he knew he had another twenty minutes or so of enough light to get back with ease.

A semblance of footsteps from somewhere behind jolted him backward. The hair on the back of his neck stood up. "Hello," he whispered. "Someone there?" He trembled, which surprised him some, his composure shaken without gates around him.

But there was nothing.

"I heard . . . heard something. I know you're there, so just show your face and we can take care of this without scaring the shit out each other. I'm harmless and not looking for trouble." Half of him was speaking to the ground, looking at what varmint might've been the culprit. The longer the silence, the more likely it was the case. But the other half waited for the gunshot.

When it became obvious there was nothing there to put him out of his misery, he turned back to the Limbos. "These bastards picked the perfect place," he said aloud. Even those who could tolerate extended periods of isolation had a line. No one knows dark until they're in the middle of the wilderness. And no one could lose their mind the way they could in that dark. Yet it was beautiful. This view in particular was unlike anything Sy had ever seen, and that included the skyline of New York City as he walked across the Brooklyn Bridge or the blue waters of St. Thomas or the River Thames in London. The sheer, unadulterated land, albeit with a scar of buildings slicing through a small area, was breathtakingly natural and untouched.

If he didn't get back to reality, his altered reality, he would never go back. This view of the world washed over him in a wave of homesickness and freedom, and he couldn't lose his composure . . . or his wits.

So he slid most of the way down to the road, as his boots did not provide enough grip to handle the terrain. Once at the bottom, he noticed how truly dark it had gotten now that he was in the shadows of the shallow valleys. Still, he took a few more minutes pacing the ground, enjoying his freedom, as brief as it might be. *If I get lost on my way, fuck it*, he thought. That was fleeting though, and he decided it was time to work his way back.

The moment he turned the corner of the hill and exposed himself to the road, the truck turned on its headlights, flooding him in light.

It must have spotted him from afar, keeping its headlights off and preying. Was that the noise he'd heard up on the hill, the land playing sound tricks, the hills and mountains throwing the acoustics around? It picked up speed as he approached the side of the road. Not an ounce of him was interested in escaping. As dark as it might have been and as possible as a getaway seemed, where would he go? He'd be dead in these lands, unprepared. And if he returned home? They'd find him back at the Limbo, and that would be that. Instead, he'd take what was coming his way now, away from everyone, away from his friends. His family. He'd prefer them not to see it, anyway. Why did they need to remember him beaten to a pulp, left to die slowly? Or cuffed and dragged into the back of the truck, watching the eyes of everyone he'd grown to love staring at him taken away, never to be seen again. Reef. Lysha. No. He'd handle it now. They would remember him the way he was, and that would be okay.

The truck slowed as it approached. Finally, it stopped in front of him, the window on the driver's side lowered an inch. "Get in."

Sy took one more look around at the world around him, then he looked back to the Limbos.

"Let's go," the voice said.

"In the cab? Or in the back?"

"Back."

Sy reached out and grabbed the door handle and hesitated for a moment before pulling it open and stepping in.

The interior wasn't a typical cop car. There were no bars or dividers. There was a computer—the first time Sy had seen one since being arrested—with Sy's face was pulled up on the screen. He looked like a child, freshly shaven, hair buzzed down as close as can be.

It was dark in the truck, but it was clear as day who was sitting in the passenger seat. Davey turned and looked back at Sy. "What the hell are you doing out here?"

"I could ask you the same." Sy's voice was angry.

"First—" the person driving said. Sy recognized the voice. Fatty Arbuckle. "*How* the hell did you get out here?"

Sy wasn't exactly owed a lawyer, but he wasn't selling out regardless. Not that easily. "I climbed the gate."

"Without getting sliced once?" Davey looked him up and down. "Impossible."

"Look," Sy said, calmly, "do what you gotta do. Just leave the rest of them alone." Sy was shocked he wasn't dead already. Having stupefied them with his escape might've bought him some time. *Dragging it out*, he thought.

Davey turned in his seat and looked Sy in the eyes. "Relax. You're safe in here."

Sy chuckled.

"Seriously, what the fuck were you doing out there? You looking to get killed?"

"Just wanted some fresh air."

"Be as sarcastic as you want, but it's not gonna matter when you go for another midnight stroll and a different LOT puts a bullet in both your legs and lets you freeze to death out here."

"That one of the moves they teach you in the LOT academy?" Sy asked. "I'm sure your training was all very professional and fair."

The fat one slammed the brakes and threw the car into park, turning around to face Sy. "Listen, who the fuck you think watches Davey's ass as he gets all the shit for you guys? Or for anyone else? You think this guy just appeared from another state and got a job at LOT headquarters, rides a dirt bike like he's been doing it for years, and pulls money and time out of his ass?" He scoffed.

Sy screwed up his face.

"Yeah, exactly. You're welcome. I'm not gonna judge you for assuming I'm a piece of shit. There are plenty of times in my life I have been a piece of shit, but I'm no murderer or racist. And neither is Davey. And you're goddamn lucky we saw your ass out here and not the next car coming."

Sy was speechless at first, but the anger hadn't completely subsided. "Am I supposed to thank you?" he asked, finally. "You're taking a hissy fit and slamming on your brakes like I'm being unreasonable. Do you understand what we've gone through over these years?"

Fatty just shook his head.

"So, yeah, thank you very fucking much for all of your help. We all appreciate the midnight raids and confiscations and punishments and such."

"You don't have the slightest idea of a

fraction of the things I've done for you guys. Who do you think is in charge of the cameras? Who keeps an eye on you? What else did you want me to? End up in there with you?"

"Maybe tell us a bit sooner," Sy said. It came out in a whisper.

"I don't care how small the community is—my spot would've been blown up in a matter of days. This alone is out of my comfort zone."

Sy just sat back.

"And I'm Leonard. Not 'Fatty' or whatever you all call me." He shifted the car into drive and pulled away quietly down the same road on which Sy had stood, past the hill and continuing on, the road curving as it got closer to the Limbos.

At certain points, the road bordered the fences, nearly touching them. Then it would swerve out for a quarter mile or so and veer back in. In plain view were all the buildings Sy could barely see from his own window. The buildings CJ had gotten a glimpse of from the rooftop that day, where he sat. And sat. And sat. Sy understood CJ now. He could've spent the night up on that hill, staring at the mountains and dirt and sky and earth until his eyes were too heavy to stay open. "Why are you doing this?"

Leonard switched on the light in the truck and held up his arm. On his forearm was a tattoo. He said it aloud as Sy tried to make out the writing: "No longer will violence be heard in your land, nor ruin or destruction within your borders, but you will call your walls Salvation and your gates Praise." He put his arm back down. "Isaiah 60:18."

"And how does a God-fearing man end up doing what you do?" Sy rephrased.

"Because we're all sinners. But watching firsthand the devastation this has caused should be enough to break anyone. Anyone decent, anyway. I made the decision not to be one of the others anymore. And never again."

The car rounded the opposite end of the complex of Limbos. Not much more than a navy blue glow to the starry sky remained. The headlights caught a random tenant here and there walking their own grounds, and for the first time, Sy realized how much they all looked like zombies. Perhaps they were. Eat when they could and wait for . . . whatever. Lives stripped, leaving only a body, and, eventually as time passed, a vague hint of a personality, if they were lucky.

Leonard pulled the truck to the side of the road about two Limbos away. "I'm gonna let you off here. Can you get back in without help?"

Davey turned to look at Sy.

"Yeah," Sy said. "As long as I have a few minutes before the next truck."

Leonard nodded.

Davey reached back and patted Sy's leg. "No one else finds out. Please. It's not a threat. It's a request. I want to keep this going, and if rumors start spreading, we'll be out of business. You get me?"

Sy nodded.

"And stay inside," Leonard said. "Please." The man looked in the rearview. He had piercing blue eyes.

"I'm not staying here forever," Sy told him. "I don't know if it'll just be me or if a few others will follow. But I refuse to die here. And when that time comes, I'll let the both of you know. I won't let it be on your watch."

Leonard only swallowed hard.

"But I have to ask you," Sy continued. "What's going to happen to my people? I have every intention of coming back for them." Sy looked out of the window at the Limbo to his right and wondered why he was opening up to this man, someone he hardly knew and who could be luring him into some twisted trap. But he pressed on. "For all of them. And then, I'm going to burn this fucking place to the ground, so that fifty years from now people won't be lining up, taking pictures of themselves on the grounds that were painted with my friends' blood. Or in the rooms where we all nearly froze to death at one point or another. Or did."

"They'll be fed. There's been a huge uptick in SLRs because of the new initiative. There'll be more food. For now."

The words shook Sy. "And the SLRs? Success rate anywhere near what they say they are?"

Neither Davey nor Leonard answered. Only

looked at each other, expressionless.

Sy put his hand on the handle of the door. "Figured as much."

"Listen, I'm not saying people haven't gotten through it," Leonard said.

Sy pulled the handle and stepped out. Before closing the door, he turned around and looked in. "I, uh . . . thanks. Thank you. It's not easy being you guys, either. Some of you, at least. I get that. I hope that one day something good comes your way."

"This *is* our good," Leonard said. "And the two of us are not the only ones."

Sy patted the seat. "See you around."

FOURTEEN

SY TRIED to find a cloud, to no avail. The sky was blue forever. Once in a while, he would hear a dirt bike in the distance. Could've been Davey. Could've been a local. Every half hour or so a truck drove by. Sy didn't bother rising to look. Neither did Lysha. She kept her head on his stomach, where it had been for at least two hours as they both fell in and out of consciousness. The 65-degree May breeze was hypnotic, and the grass more comfortable than ten Limbo mattresses stacked. Sy had rolled his thermal for a pillow.

His stomach growled and he laughed, bobbing Lysha's head up and down. That made him laugh even harder. She lifted his t-shirt and blew a raspberry on his skin.

He stroked her hair out of her face—a rare occasion, her wearing it down, but she'd just washed it and it dried naturally in the sun, her curls tightening and then dangling all over. "These work as a pillow all by themselves," he said, still running his hands through her hair.

"If I don't tie it up at night, I'll wake up clawing at my neck. So hot and itchy, and I really believe they try to strangle me."

"Forget about sweating. Might as well glue every hair to my face and neck."

She looked up at him. "You've got such thick, beautiful hair," she said. "Had you ever worn it long before here?

Long was an understatement. The only relief he got from it was when he tied it up in a knot. "No. I shaved my head for years, almost exclusively.

"Beard too?"

"Beard too."

She reached up and rubbed his face. "I bet you're even prettier under there."

He huffed. "I'm too manly to be pretty."

She blew air out through her lips.

"Ouch."

"Ah, you're tough. Getting a little scrawny lately, though." She prodded his ribs, and he jumped.

"I'm on a diet. Highly concentrated amounts of food."

She just shook her head. "Better not cut that hair when we get back to civilization."

The beard was going the first day possible, though. Davey had brought in some single-blade razors the week before. It had taken him some time to work up the trust to bring sharp objects to the camp. After all, if someone killed another prisoner—or worse yet, a guard—the first question would be where the hell they got razors from. Davey couldn't risk that. But there was another slip-up in his thinking. There couldn't be tenants walking around with fresh haircuts and shaves. Would raise some pretty big red flags. And as Sy raised the razor to his face, knowing this, it nearly took growing a third hand to stop him. God, it would feel so good. *Just shave it. They won't question one guy,* he thought. But it wouldn't be fair to everyone else. He dropped it into the sink and sat on the bed, massaging his hairy cheeks.

Fuck.

But there was someone else he might be able to appease.

"Look," Lysha said, lifting her pant leg. Her skin contrasted the green grass.

Sy whistled.

"Right! Smooth. Feel."

He caressed her leg from her calf down to her ankle. It felt like silk.

"A little ashy, but at least you won't feel like you're sleeping in bed with a man."

"I've never felt that way. Never bothered me at all." Sure it did. And this was much nicer.

A cloud finally floated above. "An eagle," Lysha said.

"Looks more like a . . . nothing. I can't really see anything."

"Not the cloud. Over there in the tree. It's an eagle."

He propped up on his elbows. "No shit. Bald isn't it? Damn near four years, and I've never seen one."

It soared to the next tree, looking around, searching for a rabbit or field mouse. Anything. Natural instinct, intimidating and awesome. From its perch, it glanced at the Limbos, the movement of tenants shuffling about catching its eye. It returned its focus to the fields, hopped to another tree, and then took off into the distance as the front gate to Limbo 5-8 slid open.

Lysha looked at Sy. "Food," he said. "Has to be." He moved to get up.

"Stay," she said. "Let them handle it."

He hesitated a moment, but plopped down onto his back. Residual dust from a rainless few days kicked up a small cloud. It settled and he inhaled deeply, taking in the day again.

Lysha stared at him, but he was far away. "What?"

"Nah, nothing. I just catch myself thinking about how many years of my life the stress of this hell hole has cost me. Cost us." He massaged his elbow. "I'm sore sometimes, like someone beat the shit out of me. Muscle aches or joint pain. Can't really tell. Joe thinks it's arthritis. Malnutrition, family history, stress. Ain't that some shit? Thirty and arthritis." He flexed his wrists. "Could be worse, I guess."

"You've never told me this."

"There are a bunch of things I've never told you."

"Oh, really?"

"We'll learn all about each other in time, won't we? No need for *more* stress. Plus, this is the fun part, anyway."

An argument from the front gate erupted. Sy listened closely, trying to determine if the yelling was playful or serious. He was on his feet and running a second later.

"Listen, you fucking nigger." A LOT with fire-red hair that Sy had never seen before was aiming his gun down at Reef's face as Reef lay flat on his back. "Ever speak to me like that again and I'll end you, you welfare piece of shit." The man had to be new—Sy had never seen him before.

"Whoa, whoa. What's going on?" Sy asked, slowing his sprint into a jog as he got closer. The LOT pulled the gun up to Sy's face, who stopped in his tracks. He put his hands out in front of him. "Just trying to figure out what's—"

"Stand the fuck back is what's going on."

A second LOT exited from his truck. Stretch. He joined the first officer. "Gentlemen. Meet Mason." Two other LOTs were unloading food from another truck. They were simply delivery officers, not nearly as high-ranking as Stretch and his new buddy.

"They were just tossing the food at us," Reef said, keeping his eyes on the LOT. "The fucking food was falling out of the boxes and onto the ground."

Sy surveyed the area around them. Three boxes lay on their sides, unopened. Two others were upside down, food contents spilled all over. Sandwiches had fallen out, into the dirt. Sections of bread had rolled feet away from the box, and a tub of peanut butter exploded upon impact with the ground, along with packages of hard-boiled eggs.

The LOT had lowered his weapon and was talking to his partner.

Sy looked to the two officers who were still unloading boxes. "Why?"

"Shut up and mind your business," Mason said, pointing. Certainly a newbie. The shake in his voice gave it away.

Another box was tossed, crashing into the few that hadn't burst apart. Sy felt a rage simmering. He tried to suppress it. The LOT holstered his weapon, and Sy took the opportunity to approach Reef. There was blood on his face. He reached down and helped him to his feet. Reef's nose gushed blood and was crooked at the bridge. "What did they do to you?"

"Pistol whipped me," Reef said through the blood on his lips. Droplets sprayed Sy in the face. He took off his shirt and held it up to Reef's nose, tilting his head forward at the same time. Not two seconds later, something heavy hit him in the back and head at the same time. He stumbled forward but didn't fall. When he turned around, he heard laughter and saw the box of food that had been hurled at him by the officers handling them.

"That's the last one," the officer said. "I didn't want it to break, so I figured I'd toss it at something soft."

Sy laughed and stood up straight.

"Seymour . . ." Lysha said from somewhere behind him. Might as well have been a mile away.

"You sign up for that?" Sy asked the officer.

"'Scuse me?"

"Delivering food for a living. That your dream growing up? Being a slave, bringing stale rice cakes to concentration camp prisoners?"

The officer strolled closer. He put his hand on his baton.

"You can pull that out and beat me with it, but that *still* doesn't change the fact that you're a glorified pizza-delivery cop. And by the looks of you, not even too glorified."

The officer was shorter than Sy by a good four inches or so. Chunky, even more so compared to Sy's emaciated body. He stepped up close, with about a foot between them. He was chewing a toothpick, switching it from side to side cockily.

"You think you intimidate me?" Sy asked.

Mason approached now. The two remaining officers, Stretch and the other driver wearing a LOT baseball cap—another heavy dude with a true 1980s burly mustache, glasses, and a shaved head, who looked more like he'd had a bread route as opposed to being a part of law enforcement—closed the distance as well.

"You bet I do. I'll bet my fat cock that I can make you piss yourself with one swing."

"Scared?" Sy ruminated and nodded. "Now, that I'll give you." He shrugged. "I'm always scared here. Scared of dying. Scared of suffering." He counted on his fingers. "Scared for my friends. Scared for my family, out there somewhere." He dropped his hand. "I've been scared from the moment I stepped foot in that truck, yeah. But I'm certainly not intimidated," he spit out. "This is our food that you threw on the ground. It's the only thing that keeps us alive. And barely. You find that amusing? How are you a human being?"

"*I'm* a human being," the short LOT said. "But you're not. You're barely even a living being. Look at you." He hocked some snot into his mouth and spat it on Sy's boot. "Pathetic. You'll be dead in a few months. Think anyone will miss you?"

Sy went on, unfazed. He glanced down at the man's left hand. "Single guy? Forty? Forty-five? Seems to me like you'd be the one forgotten. Or do you still live with Maw and Paw?"

"And they call us racist, sir," the LOT said, looking at Stretch, who now had his hand on his weapon as well.

"Sy, hon, come here," Lysha called. "Leave them. We'll figure out the food." Mateo held her back, his arm in front of her.

"I'm a bigot, you got that right," Sy said,

louder. "A bigot against stupid, which you four have a stranglehold on." He paced back and forth a bit.

"I'd quit while you're ahead, son," Stretch said.

"Yeah, you know, you keep calling me that, but the thing is, I'm not your son. My father's still out there because he picked a different team than I did. But he's not like you guys. He was able to learn from his mistake. He's the same commendable and respectful human he always has been. A lot more than can be said for you, you coward fuck."

The short LOT pulled out his baton and snapped the telescoping piece of steel into place.

Now Sy spat on the ground in front of the trooper, who immediately swung the baton and connected partially with Sy's shoulder as he turned his body in anticipation of the blow.

"No!" Lysha screamed, breaking free from Mateo and racing over to Sy. The LOT swung full-strength at Lysha's stomach. She threw her arms low to protect herself, and her forearms took the brunt of the blow. She dropped to the ground.

"Cunt," he said.

Sy rose up and exploded toward the man. He tackled the him into the fence. The officer dropped the baton and Sy put him in a chokehold. Stretch pulled his gun from its holster, followed by Mason. Mateo crept up slowly behind both of them and punted the weapon from Stretch's hands. It soared beyond all of them and rolled into the shit trench.

Mason jerked around and fired off a round impulsively, accidentally hitting Stretch in the neck, grazing him. Lysha worked herself to her feet and jumped on top of Mason, grabbing his arms before he could fire off another round. He tried to wrestle her off, but she sunk her teeth into his neck, tearing a chunk of flesh and tendon. He screamed and turned to fire again, but Reef cracked the back of his skull with a rock. The sound was hollow and deep. It was enough to knock Mason off his feet and onto all fours. Reef stepped on the officer's knuckles, and he dropped his weapon. He reached down and scooped up the gun, but Mason struggled upright and wrapped himself around Reef's body. They both fell to the ground, where they scrapped. Reef swung the gun, but Mason blocked the blow and the gun tumbled onto the dirt.

Sy squeezed the much-smaller officer's throat until he fell limp. It took much longer than it should have, but Sy finally dropped the man, unconscious, to the ground. The second delivery officer stood frozen, mustache and all, near his delivery truck. It seemed like the first action he'd faced or even seen, and he was no longer the snickering bastard who was throwing boxes of food at helpless people. Now he cowered and readied his baton. Sy gathered that neither of the officers who delivered food carried a gun, so he picked up the short LOT's baton and made a beeline for the bespectacled man, about twenty feet away. He missed with his first swing, knocking the rearview mirror off the side of the truck. The officer came back at him with his own swing but missed terribly, leaving himself wide open. Sy brought the baton down on the back of the man's skull with everything he had in him. It made a sickening thud, and the LOT fell face-first onto the ground, his baton rolling away. He writhed in agony, rolling around and holding his head. Sy was shocked the man wasn't dead. A year before, he would've split the man's head from ear to ear with that swing.

In the instant it took Sy to see that the man was still alive, he felt a sharp pain across his upper back. Stretch had regained his composure, and, still holding his neck, slammed his baton into Sy. Sy felt lightning bolts shoot through his extremities before he stumbled back near where the short LOT snoozed and then collapsed, pins and needles throughout his body. He lifted his head and pushed himself weakly up onto his hands in time to watch Mateo scream across the dirt. Sy's relief was short-lived when another strike across his shoulder blades sent waves of pain such as he'd never felt before through his body. It sent the air from his lungs, and no sound came from his open mouth. Stretch lifted the baton again and crashed it down on Sy's shoulders a second time, where he finally collapsed onto his face and then forced a roll onto his back, putting his hands up to protect himself.

"Not so tough are you now, *son?*"

Mateo dodged Reef and Mason on the ground

and launched himself at Stretch, but Stretch dodged the lunge and sent Mateo straight into the grill of the delivery truck. His forehead careened off the metal, and he fell to the ground.

Sy gasped for air. He rolled to his side and pulled himself to his knees and then to his feet, stumbling along and eventually righting himself. He could feel the tightness in his shoulders as the tissue and muscle swelled. Stretch stared and shook his head. "Wouldja just stay down, motherfucker?"

Sy thought about going for the gun. He could hear Lysha approaching again and yelled for her to stay back.

The short LOT at Sy's feet stirred and opened his eyes, seemingly confused about where he was. Sy reared back and kicked the man in his face, knocking a few teeth rogue and spraying blood across the dirt and grass. The second delivery officer had pulled himself up, sans-glasses and wits, and climbed into his truck, albeit slowly. He left a trail of blood the entire way.

"You don't give these pathetic fucks guns?" Sy asked Stretch, laughing. Mason had wrestled Reef off of him and taken out his own baton. Sy scooped up the second baton that the trooper with the dented head had dropped. He tried not to show the pain on his face, and his grimace contorted into a snarl.

"Seymour, just let them go," Lysha begged, her arms cradled to her stomach. He looked over at her, breathing heavily, his chest heaving in and out.

She was clutching her forearms, Mason's blood dripping down her chin. He shook his head. "I can't. They'll come back and kill us all."

She begged Sy with her eyes, but he turned away.

He took notice that Mason had pulled himself together and was heading toward Mason's pistol. Stretch caught him in his tracks and grabbed him by the back of his collar. He reared back and struck him on the side of his face, across his cheekbone, with the tip of the baton. Again, Mateo crashed to the ground in a heap–directly on top of the gun.

Sy crept closer to Stretch as the officer tried to pull Mateo's body away from the weapon while still keeping his eye on Sy, but Mateo, still conscious, barely, had the wherewithal to lie on top of it with all his weight.

Sy quickly glanced to his right, where the standoff between Mason and Reef was stuck in a deadlock, neither wanting to make a move on the other. Stretch swung his baton, catching Sy on his upper arm as he turned, again, to block the blow. Sy didn't feel an ounce of pain. Not then. He cocked back and railed Stretch in the ribs with his own baton. There were two pops from the tall man's ribs. He howled and grabbed his side, dropping his weapon. Sy pushed him over with his boot and turned for Mason.

Mason swung haphazardly at both Sy and Reef, trying to maintain his distance. Reef waited for his opportunity and darted forward. Mason avoided

Reef's own swing and managed to backhand his club, glancing a blow off the side of Reef's head, sending him backwards, stumbling. Sy bolted forward now and tried dodging Mason's swing, but it caught just enough of his elbow to make him stumble and fall with the momentum. Mason pounced, straddling Sy and pinning him to the ground with the baton. He tried to press it against Sy's throat, but Sy managed to sneak a hand in between the stick and his neck. He threw a wild knee into Mason's crotch and connected enough to make the man recoil. Then he swung with the baton he still carried, but Mason caught it under his arm and pulled it away from Sy, leaving Sy weaponless and exhausted. Reef snatched the red-haired LOT from behind in a full nelson, but Mason managed to shake loose while still holding both batons, and, again, Sy pushed himself to his feet. And, again, he and Reef were in a standoff with Mason.

Stretch held his ribs and coughed up some blood while he worked back onto his legs.

"Move and I'll fucking kill you." Mateo held the gun to Stretch's temple.

In one motion, Stretch smacked Mateo's gun arm and cracked him upwards in the mouth and nose with a fist. Mateo's legs buckled and the gun sailed to the ground and slid under the truck.

"Get out here, Don, you fucking pussy," Stretch yelled to the LOT who'd climbed into the truck. Mason pulled out his phone, attempting to radio backup. Sy and Reef charged the two of them.

Reef, too close for Mason to swing, wrestled the phone out of the LOT's hand. Sy speared the ailing Stretch in the ribs with his shoulder and directly into the front of the truck. More blood ejected from the tall man's mouth. He could hear Stretch's labored breath—something was wrong inside of him. Sy threw a punch, but Stretch held up his baton and Sy's knuckles connected with it. He grabbed Sy by the shoulders and headbutted him in the face. Sy, disoriented, grabbed at the air in front of him before falling to a knee. Stretch drilled a knee into Sy's face, pushing his tooth through his lip and breaking his nose. Woozy, he rocked slightly before Stretch drove a forearm across his face, tearing the tissue on his upper lip this time. Sy crashed to the dirt and stared cloudily at the group that had gathered near Building 8. Two tenants held Lysha in a bearhug, and while she squirmed and struggled to break free, it was clear that the rest of the Limbo was petrified.

The only thought Sy had as Stretch stood above him was that he wouldn't be able to protect his friends anymore. His body had given up on him, and when he looked over to Reef, dragging himself with his elbows, it wasn't much different.

"How about now, you shitbag!" Stretch screamed as Mason panted.

Sy splayed his body on the ground. He smiled through his mask of crimson and then cackled. "Kill me, then. End it." Blood sprayed from his lips with every word. He wiped at it fruitlessly with the back of his hand. "You guys feel like winners?" Sy laughed again. "This is winning?" he choked out.

Mason staggered over and raised his baton, and Sy closed his eyes. Lysha screamed. Two shots rang out.

CJ lowered the gun from the sky as Reef struggled to his feet. The only sounds were the cries of tenants and Stretch gasping for air.

Reef took the gun from CJ and moved in on the two officers, slowly. Neither knew what to do. Their severe lack of training had shown the entire time but was now on full display. They backed away, tripping on their own boots.

Sy rolled to his side and tried working his way to his feet. The blood flowed from his face, a river of red dripping onto his chest. He made his way to his knees before toppling over onto his side again. Finally, he sat up, the most he could muster. Lysha broke free and ran to him. She supported his weight from behind. Mateo wormed over next to the both of them.

Reef didn't flinch. He didn't waver. He didn't even blink. He fired twice, striking Mason in the chest both times. The man collapsed, writhed for a moment, and expired on the spot. The blood pooled under him within seconds.

"They don't even give you vests." He tutted and pulled the clip from the gun, checking to make sure there were enough bullets left. He reloaded the Glock with a loud click. All in seconds flat.

Stretch held his hands up in front of him. "Come on, now. You're already . . . in deep enough shit. The cameras are watching every move you . . . make. Backup is going to be here any second. Don't kill . . . a sheriff."

Reef laughed a sharp laugh. "*Sheriff?* Of *what?*" He stepped closer.

"Sh—sheriff of the Loyalist Organization Troopers." He backed away slowly.

"Stop. Just stop. You weren't even a security guard before this. Tell me I'm wrong."

Stretch stood quiet.

"You know what this *nigger* did? Served in the United States Army. Sent overseas during Operation Liberation and killed innocent people for his country. I'm one of you more than you are one of you."

"Hey, man, I . . . appreciate you serving."

"No. No, you don't get to say that." Reef spit blood. "You don't get to thank me."

"Look, just come back to headquarters with me," he said, clutching his aching ribs and struggling to breathe, his stridor loud and pronounced. Blood leaked from where the bullet had sliced across his neck. "I guarantee . . . I can get you out . . . of this place. I can get you . . . in with us."

Reef shot Stretch in the kneecap from just about six feet away.

"Fuck!" the man yelled as he grabbed his knee, or what was left of it, toppling to the ground.

"Should've killed us when you had a chance,"

Reef said. "Today. Last year. When we first came in. You left us here too long. Treated us like dogs. Like rats. Rats adapt. And now you reap what you sow, Stretch."

The short LOT awoke from his nap and groaned. He glanced around, trying to process everything around him. Before he could utter a word, Reef shot him in the head once as he walked by.

Stretch made a futile attempt at crawling for his truck, and Reef reached him long before he could get anywhere, shoving him back with his foot. He lay on the ground, defeated, looking up at Reef. He knew death had come for him. He was trapped, imprisoned, just like the tenants. For the last few moments of his life, he knew exactly what it was like to be one of them. And that brought Sy a moment's peace.

"This . . . is how you want to have . . . lived?" Stretch asked. "A murderer?" He glanced over and scanned the people around him. "Murderers!"

Reef's shadow cast over the length of Stretch's body. Taller. "We're not murderers. We're just surviving."

The final two gunshots rang out into the silence.

Lysha hugged Sy gently and guided him up to his feet. It took a few tries, but he managed to get his legs under him and, one after the other, force himself over to his building as the rest of the Limbo made their way over. Joseph was one of them. He approached Sy, alarmed. Sy made an about-face and started toward Reef, stumbling a bit but gaining his footing and working himself into a limp. Reef caught him in his peripheral vision and turned to meet him. They embraced in the middle of the grass, both leaning into each other's weight. Sy put his hand on the side of Reef's face and looked him in the eyes. "Thank you." Reef closed his eyes and the tears erupted. "I'm sorry you had to do that," Sy said.

"I'm not," Reef said, barely audible.

Joseph reached Sy. "Let's get you both inside and check you out."

Sy leaned on the doctor's shoulder. "Just give me a minute." He glanced up at the crowd of a few dozen who'd gathered around. Most gasped at the bodies on the ground. Some gasped at Sy. A few cheered softly, proud of the dead LOTs on the ground, not thinking about what the future might bring. Perhaps not caring. Others cried and held their significant others, or others in general. Alma stood stoically, as if she'd seen it all before. Sy cleared his throat. It hurt to even to do that.

"Everyone, listen." His voice was breaking. "Listen to me." The chatter remained.

"Shut up and listen!" CJ snapped. Everyone fell silent.

Sy blinked, the dust stinging his eyes. "We're going to figure this out. For now, everyone needs to stay calm and be reasonable. I know that sounds ridiculous with . . ." He winced ". . . them. But I promise all of you that you'll be safe. You have my word." Chandra stared at him from the front door of Building 8. Sejal hid behind her. "Today is a different day. Today is the day we stood up for ourselves. Maybe that means we had to sacrifice ourselves for it." He looked at Reef. "Maybe that's okay. Word will spread. There." He pointed at Limbo 1-4, where people were standing at their fence looking in. Some of them, too, cheered. "Beyond them to the others on our compound. And to everyone else. It'll get out into the world that these criminals won't hold us here forever. And if we have to take the brunt of it, so be it. I'm willing to die for you. For all of you."

A dirt bike roared in the distance.

"Please, try not to panic. We'll handle this. For now, go home, carry on. Food'll be distributed as normal. But for now, go home. Trust me. Please." Most started to walk away, uneasy but seemingly to indeed trust Sy's words.

He dropped to a knee and supported himself with a hand on the ground. The dirt bike drew nearer.

FIFTEEN

"It's DAVEY," Reef said.

"Thank God," said Mateo, holding the side of his face. The baton had hit him, but he turned his face quickly enough to avoid the full brunt of the swing. "Listen, Reef, I tried to help. I tried—"

"I know," Reef interrupted.

Mateo looked embarrassed.

"Hey," Reef said, Mateo looking up at him. "You saved our lives by guarding that gun."

Mateo shook his head.

"You saved our lives, my brother." Reef put his hand on the young man's shoulder. "Thank you."

Davey pulled up to the fence and looked in. "Well, that's something. You guys fucking took out McConnell? Shit. They're gonna wonder what happened to him."

Reef looked curiously at both Sy and Davey. Sy stumbled to the fence.

"Holy hell, you need to be tended to, man."

"In time," said Sy. "We need to fix this."

"No, now," Lysha said from behind him. Joseph was next to her. He took Sy by the arm.

"I tried to get here as fast as I could," Davey said. "Leonard called to let me know what was going on." He scanned the area. "Go into one of the trucks," he instructed Reef. "Find 'Gate 5-8' on the screen and touch 'open'."

Reef approached the truck and suddenly remembered the fourth LOT. He drew the gun he'd taken from Mateo and aimed it at the vehicle. He rounded the door and pulled it open, pointing the weapon in the cab. Don was there, leaning against the wheel, dead. He'd bled out from his head wound.

Reef did what he was told, and the gate hummed open. Davey pulled inside. "Grab me the radio. Then go get the one from McConnell's truck." Reef tossed the radio from inside the food delivery truck to Davey as Davey climbed off his bike. Reef did the same from the other truck, and Davey stuffed the radios into the slats of the fence, picked up a baton, and smashed them to pieces. He took the pieces, paced over to the shit trenches, and tossed them in.

Upon returning, he muttered "GPS" and searched the bodies and the area around them for their phones. He collected all four and smashed them as well. He pulled out his phone and dialed a number. "Yeah, it's a clean-up on aisle 5. McConnell went and got himself perished." He paused. "Oh, definitely dead." He kicked at McConnell's body. "All four. Biggest so far. Okay. Hour." He ended the call and stuffed the phone into his pocket. "Mateo, go empty out the back of that truck. Take whatever food you guys want. Matter of fact, take all of it, empty it out for me. Get a few to help you." Mateo and CJ had already jumped into action.

"What about everyone else?" Sy croaked, being led by Joseph to the front of the building. "That's their food. 1-4. 9-12."

"They'll get food. Leonard will send out another food truck as soon as he can. They'll think the four LOTs went AWOL and abandoned duty. Good luck finding them."

"And the bodies?" Mateo asked, box in hand.

"Where Davey threw the radios," Sy answered before Davey could. "Where they belong."

"You're good, you," Davey said.

"So far?" Sy asked, leaning on Joseph.

"What?"

"You said the biggest so far, on the phone with Leonard."

"You think you guys are the only ones who've killed a LOT?

"Who the fuck is Leonard?" Reef interrupted.

Davey looked over at Sy.

"No." Sy answered the telekinetic question. "I didn't tell anyone."

"Tell us what?" Reef was agitated.

"Leonard is the big guy," Sy said. "You know

who I'm talking about."

"Fat-ass?"

"Yeah. He's a good one."

"Good one?"

"He's one of the LOTs in charge of cameras. He scooped me up that night, up on the hill out there."

Reef recoiled in confusion.

"I told you I just hid and then took the long way back to avoid being seen? Well, it was Leonard and Davey in the truck. They picked me up and brought me back. There's a reason we haven't gotten in any shit from the cameras watching us. Davey has been a fucking soldier. And Leonard is a good dude. Anyone who Davey vouches for in my book is someone we can trust." Sy winced again. "Let's get the bodies out of here first."

"No," Lysha said. "You're going inside."

"She's right," Reef said. "Get your ass in and let him patch you up. We'll handle this."

"And your nose?"

"Already took care of it."

Sy grimaced. He looked at Davey, who nodded.

"Once Leonard gets here, we'll take the trucks and drive them somewhere they won't be found," said Davey. "Then we'll burn 'em out. We'll do the same to the bodies once they're in the trenches. Leonard will keep track of the routes and we'll time it right. We'll be fine. Go get taken care of."

Sy relented and limped, with the help of Joseph, into Building 8, passing the few tenants who remained, trying to soak in the situation. Alma brushed his arm with her hand as he walked by. He stopped and looked into her eyes. Her smile lines ran deep. She took him by the hand, leaned in, and kissed Sy on his cheek, smiling again before walking away. He held her hand as long as he could. When she was out of reach, he entered the building and made for his room, where he sat gingerly on his bed. He breathed deeply, painfully, and his ears rang from the silence.

Chandra peeked in.

"Are you okay, Seymour?"

Sy smiled an ugly smile. "I'll be okay." The blood continued to drip from his mouth. Sejal stared at him. "It's okay, sweetie." He tried to smile at her, but the expression felt distorted. He turned away. "It's just my lip. Doctor Joseph is going to fix me up all new. Then we'll play hide and seek again. Okay?"

She nodded. "You killed the men. Well, Shariyf did."

"Yeah," Sy said. "We did."

"I know that they're dead, just like Siva."

"Not like Siva," Sy corrected. "Siva died because of them. And we're trying to stop them from doing that to any more people."

"But they're still dead, just like Siva."

He sighed deeply. "You're not wrong."

Lysha appeared in the doorway, standing behind them. She caressed the top of Sejal's head.

Chandra thanked them again and took Sejal away with her. "Hide and seek later," Sejal yelled back.

"You bet." Sy hugged himself. "Fuck me. This hurts."

Joseph pulled up Sy's wooden chair. "I need you to lean over the sink and let me rinse your face so I can see what the damage is."

Sy closed his eyes and obliged. He clenched his teeth as the doctor wiped away the drying blood from his lips and nose, looking for where the lacerations began and ended. "Stitches in both lips. Broken nose." He patted Sy's face clean with a paper towel and then lay him on his back, gently, and felt his ribs. "Ribs seem okay. Tender there?" he asked.

"No."

"How about here?" He felt the other side.

"A little. Nothing horrible."

He felt Sy's chest and neck, and then moved on to his upper right arm. Sy squealed, pinching his eyes shut and nearly folded in half. It was already purple and blue where the redheaded LOT had struck him relentlessly with the baton. "I don't think he broke anything. Just a hell of a contusion. A bone bruise. We have to keep an eye on it. We don't want compartment syndrome there." Joseph continued down Sy's arm and to his hand, which was swollen and purple as well. He tried to move a few fingers, and Sy pulled his hand away forcefully.

"Fuuuuuuck. It's broken." He held it in the

pit of his stomach with his other hand.

"Give it to me," the doctor said. Sy looked at him and reluctantly placed his hand in Joseph's. The man squeezed it in a few places, searching for the break, then squinted out into the distance, concentrating on what he was feeling. "I think I found it. Here, bite on this." He handed Sy more paper towels.

Lysha leaned in close and took Sy's other hand. "Squeeze my hand if you need to."

Sy pulled it away. "I'll break your goddamn hand if I do that." He gripped the side of the mattress. "Go."

Sy screamed, and the doctor paused. As quickly as he'd stopped, he started again, applying even more pressure. Finally, he was finished. "It's probably a fracture. Nothing is out of place from what I can feel," said Joseph. "We're going to have to stabilize it, somehow." Sy opened and closed his hand. "Don't do that. You might offset it. The ligaments around it can swell and pull. I'll see if I can come up with something to keep everything in place. But keep it stable. Now flip onto your stomach."

"Kinky," Sy gritted through his teeth.

"Flip."

Sy took a deep breath, filling his lungs to capacity. He let it out slowly and flipped over onto his stomach with a pitiful groan. The movement made his lip and nose bleed some more. Lysha hissed at the sight of his back. More specifically, his shoulder blades. Joseph explored with his hands. Sy looked as if he were going to pass out. "Just a little more," Joseph said.

"My back hurts when I breathe," Sy volunteered. "Deep breaths only." He took one and winced. "Yeah."

"Your scapula may be fractured. Are you having any trouble breathing apart from that?"

"No."

"I'll need to know if you're getting chest pains or heaviness or having trouble breathing. I can't do much in the way of its healing. Has to do that on its own. We can sling you up, keep it immobile. But it's like ribs. Just needs to heal."

"Okay." Sy sat gingerly and lifted the legs of his pants. Blood dripped from his lips onto his skin. His legs were bruised and swollen. "Fuckin' asshole." He rubbed the egg on the side of his knee. "If my kneecap is broken, I'm going to shoot him again."

"One thing at a time," Joseph said. "Let's make sure your internal organs are okay and stitch up your face while we're at it. I'm going to go get some supplies. Don't . . . move."

Sy agreed sarcastically. "Thanks, Doc."

Lysha slinked down onto the edge of the mattress, looking down at her forearms, bruised already, hopefully nothing more. She examined Sy pitifully.

"I'm okay," he said, muffled.

"Are you?"

"I will be. Are you?"

She shook her head.

"I'm sorry."

"So am I." She kissed his head.

Sy admired her for her dedication, and then her bruises. "Thank you for protecting me."

"Protecting *you?*" she asked, exasperated. She burst into tears, her face in Sy's hair. He could feel her breath on his scalp as she sobbed.

When Joseph returned with a small brown bag, he found Sy resting his eyes. "Sorry, kiddo. We have to do this now. Your buddy is outside, by the way."

"Who?" Sy asked, moving his arms to loosen up. The aching pain was already setting in.

"The LOT. The heavy one. He asked about you. He's with Davey, trying to figure out their next move, I think."

Sy wanted to be out there. "Once I'm stitched up, I'll go talk to them."

Lysha stepped forward. "Sy, I don't think . . ." She stopped. "You need to rest."

Joseph pulled out a bottle of rubbing alcohol, a pack of sewing needles, and sutures from his pocket. He produced a bottle of ibuprofen from his other pocket and spilled four capsules into his palm. "Open up."

Lysha handed Sy a cup of cold water. He sipped it carefully, and the water in the cup tinged red with blood. He swallowed all four pills at once.

"This is going to suck," Sy said.

"It is," Joseph said. "But we'll get through it."

Sy, again, gripped the sides of the mattress as Joseph dipped the needle in rubbing alcohol. He'd also poured the alcohol into a cup and dropped the sutures in.

Lysha looked pale. "You're turning into a white girl," Sy mumbled.

"No, I'm okay." The degree to which her voice drifted higher from her typical octave was obvious. It made Sy laugh, and she laughed back for the first time. Their eyes connected. "I'm okay." He said it in earnest.

She rubbed his forehead. "But you almost weren't."

"We're all almost not, almost all the time." The swelling of his lips inhibited the words. "We're safe right now."

"Ready?" Joseph asked.

"Go for it." He closed his eyes. When the doctor was done, he poured fresh rubbing alcohol onto Sy's lips as Sy hung his head over the sink again. It was the only time Sy made a sound during the entire stitching. He grunted and had to lean against the wall, the pain making him lightheaded. The pain elicited every response in the area. He wiped tears from his eyes, and his nose ran with clear snot. He rinsed his face in the sink, and the doctor patted it dry.

"Take these," Joseph said, holding up a bottle. "One in the morning and one at night. Prophylactic. Ten days. Don't stop or skip."

Sy took the bottle, popped one into his mouth, and put the rest on the windowsill. He swallowed with a sip of water and turned for the door.

"Sy, please," Lysha begged.

He turned to her. "I'll be right back, I promise. I'm not hanging out. Just seeing what's going on. I'll be right back. Joseph, please look at her arms while I'm gone."

He passed Mateo in the common room, seated on the floor with his back against the wall. The adjacent wall was stacked nearly to the ceiling with boxes of food. He acknowledged the man's hard work as Mateo stared in awe at seeing Sy on his feet, walking around. He pushed through the front door and the sun hit him in the face as it lowered in the sky. He limped around the side of the building and found Reef and Davey next to one of the LOT trucks.

"The hell you doing out here?" Reef asked. "Go lie down. We got it."

"I'm okay," Sy said, his words still muffled. "The meds are kicking in."

Davey stared at him in disbelief. "You look worse than McConnell."

Sy kicked some dirt over the bloodstained ground. "Where're the bodies?"

"The trench," Davey responded. "Soon to be carbon. Leonard took the other truck to get some gasoline."

"What'll he do with that truck after he's done?" Reef asked.

"Drive it far away, remove any kind of identification, and burn it. They won't find it. They won't even try to find it. It'll be a charred hangout in the woods for squirrels and teenagers smoking weed. Same for this one."

"Thanks for being here for us," Sy said.

Davey shook his head.

"Now go rest, Sy," said Reef. "Please. We got this."

Sy held his hand up in concession and turned slowly. He hobbled away from the two men, kicking up dirt as he dragged his sore leg behind him slightly. But he didn't walk straight to the building. Instead, he made his way to the trenches. As he approached the edge of the earth where it dropped deep down into the filth and excrement pit, and where the smell hit you long before you got there, the gravity of the situation finally draped him in a heaviness that weighed him down and brought out the pain he'd been masking. The adrenaline was gone, and his legs were weak. His arms were weak. His head pounded. His face hurt. His body hurt. His *being* hurt.

He peered over the edge and saw them. All four bodies dumped, one over the other, into the man-made hole, twisted into angles and positions that would make a contortionist look away. Their faces, if not blown mostly away by gunshot, were just as gnarled. And they'd remain that way until the underground funeral pyre melted them away.

Sy closed his eyes. "I'm sorry."

The walk back to Building 8 hurt every step of the way, and had he not been so close, he might've collapsed. But just as he finally reached the door and grasped the knob, the speakers in the courtyard came to life, playing their decrepit version of the National Anthem. Sy dropped his hand and stumbled over to them, looking up at the speakers like they were a screen, ready to display what was coming next.

Halfway through the song, a familiar laugh interrupted. The same laugh as last time.

"Hello. Us again.

"It's been awhile. Sorry we haven't spoken sooner, but we had to make sure they weren't tracking us. We need all the anonymity we can muster, but we want to make sure you know where we are. We mentioned city halls and libraries last time, but we'll do you one better. We're moving into every capital and every major city. Every one. Look for a blue wrist band, anywhere you can find one. Don't be fooled by an intercept. We are discreet, but there will always be traitors. This you should know by now. Distinguish us by our faces and ask us what you know we'll know. And what they won't.

"And during the next LOT raid, give them the middle finger for us."

The speakers screeched off. For the first time, no one else was outside for the announcement. But

247

Sy knew they were listening.

He walked back and turned the knob with a pained expression. Before pushing it open, he peered around the corner of the building again, to Reef and Davey. They stopped talking and looked back at him.

"Guys, when you burn the bodies, will you torch the entire trough? Please. Just this once."

Davey nodded.

"Thanks." He entered, and closed the door behind him.

SIXTEEN

LYSHA KISSED Sy on his scar—the one on his bottom lip. It was still red, though healed. He pulled her in tightly and squeezed. They both looked into his room. It was an odd sight, empty and even colder than normal. The mattress was noticeably misshapen from the years of weight. Certain spots were flat to the metal underneath. Sy pulled a folding knife from his pocket and opened it. He stepped up to the bed and sliced the mattress down the middle. Cotton protruded like the innards of an animal. He closed the knife and returned it to his pocket.

They both stepped into the common area. It was also bare, stripped of all food and supplies. There wouldn't be anyone left to use them. Outside, Reef stood with Chandra, Sejal, and Santi, all of their supplies on their backs. Reef's shaven face and short hair were still jarring for Sy, though his own beardless chin felt good. And seeing nearly everyone else in 5-8 so clean and groomed felt good, too.

"The rest get a head start?" Sy asked, adjusting his own pack.

"All of 'em," Reef confirmed.

"The others still staying behind?" Sy tied his hair high on his head with a rubber band.

"Steadfast," Reef said, disappointed.

Joseph was one of the very few who'd chosen to remain. "There are others here who will need me," he told Sy the night before, while removing Sy's microchip in the doctor's own bedroom. Over the week or so leading up to the departure from Limbo 5-8, Joseph had removed everyone's chips, everyone who was planning to go. They were disposed of in the shit trench. After the surgery, Sy and the doctor played some hands of rummy. "I can't leave them behind. The older ones. Alma. The sickly ones. They'll die. You? You'll make it. And there will be many more doctors out there."

"Doctor Joe they'll never be, though," Sy said. He shook his head. "I'm damn sad you won't be beside us. And I'll miss the hell outta you. But I respect what you're doing. You know that."

"I do know. And I respect you for everything you've done. And are doing. You're a good man."

"We'll find out." Sy and the doctor embraced in a hug. "I'll be back for you. And the rest. I promise."

"Don't doubt it."

"Good. Until then, Davey and Leonard will keep an eye on things. I'll be in touch with them. You need anything, let them know."

Joseph didn't come outside for goodbyes. It was better that way.

"You got your phone, yeah?" Reef asked, holding up his own. "They're loaded with prepaid minutes. I didn't even know they did that anymore, but Davey got them for us."

Sy held up his phone. "You called each one to test the numbers, correct?" Sy asked.

"Yes. We can't break these damn things or we'll be shit out of luck staying in touch. Won't know if you get where you're going or if I get up there safely."

Up there.

When Reef approached a healing Sy to tell him he was ready to go, Sy had interrupted him before he could say anything. "September," Sy said.

"We need to convince everyone we can to come with us." Reef sat.

"What if they refuse?"

"We can't force them. But I don't know what the LOTs will do once they find this place half empty."

"Probably laud them for staying put," said Sy. "Then patch the fence and move on. At least we have Leonard to make sure they'll be taken care of."

Reef stood again, clearly uncomfortable, his brain on overload. He paced with his hands folded across his chest. "Can we be sure Leonard and Davey are enough to watch out for them?"

"We have to be okay with it. For those who don't come along, we'll have them rat us out. Show them the hole in the fence and make it look like they had no interest in coming along."

"So we're doing this," Reef said, more to himself than Sy.

"I've been doing this since I first knocked that rung loose. And I can't tell you how happy I am you'll be coming with me."

"Come on, man. I knew twenty minutes after we talked about it I'd be in. Just had to figure out I knew. Pray on it. Been praying on it for months. There was no way I was letting you get all the glory." He punched Sy in the shoulder.

Sy laughed hard, wincing at the pain. "You'll have your glory." His face changed. He frowned. "You're still going to Canada?"

Reef acknowledged this with his silence.

"Look, I don't blame you. If you feel that's the right move, I support it."

"I've tossed it back and forth for a while. You know that," said Reef. "I just don't want to be here anymore. There's nothing left for me. There was nothing left before they brought me here. A fucking black Muslim veteran. Soon on the run. A fugitive. A murderer."

"You're far from a murderer."

"Nothing but a murderer. If I never have to shoot a gun again—"

"You will if you have to," Sy interrupted. "Just promise me that."

Reef simply stared into the distance.

They moved one at a time, out of sight of the cameras. Habit. It was overcast. Gloomy. The air was damp and sticky. "If you're in trouble. If you're second-guessing yourself. If you're . . ."

"I know," said Reef. "I will. I'll call. And you'll do the same."

Sy looked at Chandra and the kids. "You guys ready to leave?" Their expressions weren't excited, but rather stoic. The children had lived a large portion of their lives in Limbo. Grown up there. Both children had been hardened by life in a camp but now were about to walk into the unknown, and in many ways, they were no longer children at all. The excitement was reserved for the adults. Even Chandra was optimistic.

"Everyone, don't forget your checkpoints," said CJ. "Every fifty miles. Every seventy-two hours, minimum. Leave a message if the phone is off, which it should be. All phones on at 8 p.m. to check for messages, text or otherwise."

"Roger that," Sy responded. "Did I say that right?"

"Good enough. You've got everything rationed and portioned for the two of you?" Reef asked.

"I took care of all of it," Lysha said. She was

dressed for the warm weather, and Sy couldn't help fawning over her. She was stunning, no matter what. Funny, he'd never seen her with an ounce of makeup, or heels, or a fancy dress, and she was absolutely more stunning than anyone he'd ever been with. "And the others are all ready to go," she continued. "Maps packed. Tents ready and enough for everyone. We'll be to Denver likely before you guys get to the border. We'll fill you in on everything going on there as soon as we can."

"Don't forget your phones have GPS and your solar chargers will make sure you always have juice," Reef reminded Sy and Lysha. "Still, know your maps. The real ones, not the ones made of crayon that Sy drew up. Stay away from the LOT routes, but don't rely on that completely. Keep your eyes peeled for them. And not just them, but anyone who might call them. If you see people, assume they aren't friendly."

"At least you guys have CJ," said Sy. "He'll interpret that map like a smartphone. It's like having built-in GPS." He looked over toward the front of the compound. "Davey and Leonard are saints."

It had begun to drizzle, and the drops of rain pitter-pattered on the leaves and late-blooming flowers.

"What's the exact mileage to Denver?" Reef asked.

"Three hundred and forty, give or take a few."

"Yeah, you'll be there before us," Reef

confirmed.

"At least you'll know if our gamble pays off by the time you get to the border."

"Our gamble is that they're still going to take us. They turn us around or—worse—hand us over, we're fucked."

Sy craned his neck to the building behind him, then across the fenced-in grounds, pointing with his eyes.

"I know," Reef said. "I know."

"Let's get the hell out of here. Before we have to wait again."

All of them squeezed through the fence as Reef held it open. He followed after Lysha passed through and stood up straight on the other side. The drizzle turned to a steadier rain, and Shariyf smiled large. He looked at Sy. "I didn't understand how you felt that night in February. I imagined it, but I couldn't feel it."

The two of them hugged tightly, tears in their eyes. "I love you, brother," Sy said into Reef's ear.

"I love you too. You take care of yourself. And take care of each other."

Lysha hugged Reef while Sy hugged Chandra. "You take care of them. We'll see you again." He took Lysha by the hand.

"Damn right," Shariyf said.

Sy watched as Shariyf turned and guided the others in their planned direction. Within a few minutes, they'd disappeared from sight, and Lysha and Sy began their own journey.

As they walked past, Sy noticed the tenants in Limbo 1-4 staring at them through the fences. Their faces were gaunt and ghostly, their expressions hopeless. Adrenaline coursed through Sy's body as the anger filled him. *I'll be back for you all,* he thought as he walked by. Then he stopped in his tracks. Lysha stopped in response. "All of you. I'll be back for you all," he said aloud.

Their faces remained the same. Zombies.

Even when the gunshots came.

At first, they sounded from the opposite way. From where Shariyf and the rest had gone. Sy's heart raced, and he turned to grab Lysha. That's when her chest exploded on him, dousing him in blood. He looked down and then back at her as she fell forward into a heap on the ground, revealing the LOTs behind her. Two of them. Then he felt the pain in his side. The bullet had hit him, as well. He stumbled back into the fence and toppled down on all fours. He crawled forward, reaching for Lysha.

Once he could no longer move himself any farther, he glanced up at the gun in his face and watched as the LOT started to squeeze the trigger.

SEVENTEEN

JUST AS Seymour began sleeping more than an hour at a time in his new bed, another prisoner arrived at Limbo 5-8. He was also shoved out of the back of the truck—a rite of passage. But, this man, like Seymour, had managed to keep his balance, though he didn't look back. Didn't give them the satisfaction. Instead, he'd forged ahead, stone-faced, head shaved short like everyone else, face with a few days' worth of stubble. He'd marched forward to the group.

Seymour stood behind CJ. They both brought the man to Building 8. CJ read the card aloud. "Shariyf. Room 4. Here you go. This is it, on the right."

"Better than most of the bunks I've slept in," he said.

"Military man?" Seymour asked.

"Army."

"Thanks for serving." He regretting saying it as soon as it came out of his mouth. "You know what I mean."

Shariyf laughed. "Appreciate it."

He noticed Shariyf's shirt—an Arabic character. "I'm Seymour." He held his hand out and Shariyf shook it.

Two months later, as they tossed wood chips into the shit trenches, along with sticks and leaves and whatever else they could use to cover the waste and the rancid smell, strong enough to burn your nostrils, the enlarged sun, sitting on the horizon, was setting. It cast an orange glow over everything.

"Reef, why'd you serve?"

Reef thought about it for a few seconds. "I think my instincts had me do it. Something just didn't smell right." He glanced down at the trench and raised his eyebrows. "My college degree was useless in Indiana. In that climate? I might as well have been invisible. I thought, hey, maybe something terrible could be coming down the pipeline. Not this, exactly." He gestured at the excrement. "But things had already started to happen, with the Mexican detainments and all that. Once the special investigation was done and it shit the bed, I knew nothing would fix this anytime soon. So I thought maybe I'd get some brownie points. Shit, I'd been in Indiana my entire life. It was time to get out anyway.

"Instead, I got sent to Palestine in the first wave."

"You were there?" Sy asked, aghast.

"A year. Once the Islamic State poured in, we

weren't leaving."

Sy spread more wood chips along the trench. He noticed George emptying his bucket at the far end and looked away from the contents falling into the ground. "Were you Muslim before you went in?"

Reef shook his head.

"Oh." Sy stopped what he was doing. "I'm the opposite. I was never a real devout Jew, but I definitely thought I believed in something. Until I ended up here. It was a slow realization, but, thinking back, I don't think I ever really did believe in anything."

"I get it." Reef kept scooping the wood chips.

He doesn't want to share it with me. And that's okay, Sy thought.

"Where does your family come from?" Reef asked.

"Ashkenazi Jew. Russian and some German, as far as I'm aware. But who knows?"

"I shot a Palestinian boy in the face."

Sy forgot what he was about to say.

Reef continued, his face exhibiting very little expression. "I watched him die. I didn't know Arabic and I didn't know he was screaming for us to help take the bomb off his little body."

"Oh, God."

"My lieutenant did, though. We had an Arabic-speaking soldier who could translate there with us the entire time. But my lieutenant still gave the order to shoot. And I did." Reef disappeared behind his eyes. "I heard him screaming, but I was instructed to fire. So I did what I was instructed to do. Protect my brothers. Then they detonated the bomb while it was still strapped to him. They didn't want to take any chances.

"I never took my eyes of off him. I killed him, so I deserved it. In Arabic, he screamed, 'Help me, I have a bomb! Get it off of me!'"

"Are you sure the boy wasn't just trying to lure you guys closer?"

"No, I wasn't sure. It'd happened before. But the look on the translator's face was all the confirmation I needed. I knew he had told my lieutenant to wait, but the bastard gave the order anyway. And you don't ask questions. You do what they say." Reef's voice was now pained, his brow furrowed.

"The boy still follows me everywhere. I see him as he was, young, playing with his friends before the extremist pricks got their hands on him. I see him as an adult, married to his wife and playing with his kids in some peaceful state. I see him with his head blown to pieces." He breathed deeply, readying himself for more words. "I see the chaos he represented, with Palestine now defunct. I studied and still study the Quran for him. I don't even feel it's me that prays. I'm just repenting. The prayers are for him. From him. I live my life for him."

As Sy listened, the wind picked up, moving limbs and branches, kicking around leaves and dirt.

"I died with him in the desert that day," Reef said. "The person I was died. Now he lives through me, through who I am today."

"Were you ever in a firefight again?" Sy asked.

"Yes, and I killed more. Some who deserved it, I guess." He crossed his arms in front of his chest. "I just imagined they were the ones who sent the boy to us. It was easy after that. Until I left. Coming home to a country that was sending innocent civilians to internment camps. Then it wasn't easy anymore." He was no longer looking at Sy, but beyond him, into the mountains. "It got harder. And harder. Loud noises. Crowds. Eventually, I could barely go outside. It was like someone was watching me, hovering over me with a blanket, draping me, trying to suffocate me. I thought it was the boy. I thought he was haunting me. Then I thought it was a jinn—a, uh, demon. I tried meditation. Yoga. The gym. Church. Medication. Everything. And no matter what, my gun was always loaded and waiting for me." He grimaced subtly. "Until I went to a mosque. Until that little child became a part of me.

"That's the only way I get by."

Sy could barely speak. "I'm sorry you had to experience that. And I wish there was more I could say. Just know you'll always have an ear. Or even silence, if that's what you need."

The sun had lowered considerably, and the orange glow began to fade.

"Thank you."

They both stared at the sunset. And when the orange was gone, and their eyes adjusted, the moon and stars illuminated the land. And Sy knew the sun would rise again. And, somehow, he knew Reef did too.

ACKNOWLEDGEMENTS

This story started out as a NaNoWriMo (National Novel Writing Month) challenge. I hadn't put out any kind of work in a little over three years, at the time, and wanted a nice little challenge. Now, nearly a year later, it's become, to me, one of the most important things I've ever written.

I'm not sure where on the spectrum of politics you might land, but that's really irrelevant. The state of today's political landscape is terrifying, beholden to the current United States White House, Senate, Supreme Court, and those who support the aforementioned. We, as a race, cannot sit back and watch as those who support these megalomaniacs bask in the glory of the demise of the country and celebrate this danger to the world political landscape, and humanity as a whole.

Vote.

Vote.

Vote.

A sincere thank you to those who helped out on this manuscript. My wife, first, for letting me cut into the little quiet time we get together to go off into la-la land to make pretend (and, sometimes, not so pretend). Your patience is unmatched and your heart humongous and beautiful.

My kids for believing me when I sit on my laptop and say, "I'm working."

Jondavid—a god amongst men. Your influence is felt throughout, not only in your medical expertise, but in your natural ability to help people. You're a role model for many. Thanks for always being a friend when I need one.

Heyler, my brother. Thanks for correcting my Spanish, helping me move a thousand boxes of books in a blizzard, and driving 18 hours in a Honda Civic coupe so I could play out a movie ending in real life.

Francesco, thanks for being my writing buddy. It's fun to vent about shit that most others wouldn't quite understand. Keep up your drive and mission, you positive pally.

Dom, for being a damn great friend and supporting a career change at 30—and helping me get through it without losing my shit.

Silas and Trapper for pressing buttons with your noses and stepping on my return key and spacebar. Couldn't have rewritten accidentally deleted parts without guys.

Justin Mermelstein
9/2/2019, New Jersey